What's the matter with Storm?

"I'm going to test him and all the other horses at Whitebrook for equine infectious anemia," Dr. Smith said slowly.

Cindy froze. Her mind was spinning with terror. She felt as if a deep hole had just opened up and swallowed her in its blackness.

Storm pulled his head from her limp fingers, but Cindy couldn't make herself move to get him back. She could only watch while Ian and Len restrained the colt so that Dr. Smith could take a blood sample. Storm rolled a pleading eye in her direction and wiggled away from the needle.

"Easy, boy," Cindy said automatically. As if in a dream she walked to Storm's side, steadying the colt with her hands and her voice. Storm relaxed at Cindy's touch, turning his head to make sure where she was. Cindy moved close so that the colt c___ see and smell her and so she could run both h_____ his warm, satiny gray neck.

"I'll have the results first thing i_____ Dr. Smith put the blood sample i_____ the other horses."

Cindy shook her head, w_____ that she hadn't heard those words. L_____ _ks all the horses are sick, she realized. Are they _____ g to die?

Don't miss these exciting books from HarperPaperbacks!

Collect all the books in the THOROUGHBRED series:

#1 A Horse Called Wonder

#2 Wonder's Promise

#3 Wonder's First Race

#4 Wonder's Victory

#5 Ashleigh's Dream

#6 Wonder's Yearling

#7 Samantha's Pride

#8 Sierra's Steeplechase

#9 Pride's Challenge

#10 Pride's Last Race

#11 Wonder's Sister

#12 Shining's Orphan

#13 Cindy's Runaway Colt

#14 Cindy's Glory

#15 Glory's Triumph

#16 Glory in Danger

#17 Ashleigh's Farewell

#18 Glory's Rival

#19 Cindy's Heartbreak

#20 Champion's Spirit

#21 Wonder's Champion

#22 Arabian Challenge

#23 Cindy's Honor*

#24 The Horse of Her Dreams*

THOROUGHBRED Super Editions:

Ashleigh's Christmas Miracle

Ashleigh's Diary

Ashleigh's Hope

Samantha's Journey

*coming soon

THOROUGHBRED

CINDY'S HEARTBREAK

CREATED BY
JOANNA CAMPBELL

WRITTEN BY
KAREN BENTLEY

HarperPaperbacks
A Division of HarperCollins*Publishers*

HarperPaperbacks
A Division of HarperCollins*Publishers*
10 East 53rd Street, New York, N.Y. 10022-5299

This is a work of fiction. The characters, incidents, and
dialogues are products of the author's imagination and are not to
be construed as real. Any resemblance to actual events or
persons, living or dead, is entirely coincidental.

ISBN 0-06-106489-0

HarperCollins®, 🔥®, and HarperPaperbacks™
are trademarks of HarperCollins*Publishers* Inc.

First printing: March 1997

Printed in the United States of America

❖ 10 9 8 7 6 5 4 3

To John

CINDY MCLEAN SETTLED HERSELF IN THE SADDLE AND gripped Wonder's Champion's cold reins tightly, shivering as a frosty breeze cut right through her denim jacket. It was Thanksgiving Day, and hard winter had set in early this year in Kentucky. "Ready to get out there on the track?" she asked the colt.

The mahogany-colored yearling turned his head to eye her mischievously, his almost black mane and tail floating behind him as he crabstepped and pranced. Cindy pointed him firmly toward the gap of the training track, where Ashleigh Griffen, her husband, Mike Reese, and Ian McLean waited at the rail. Ashleigh and Mike were co-owners of Whitebrook Farm, the Thoroughbred breeding and training farm near Versailles, where Cindy and her family lived. Ian McLean, Cindy's father, was head trainer at Whitebrook.

Cindy had exercise-ridden Wonder's Champion since this past September, when she'd been the first ever on the colt's back. At thirteen years old, Cindy had a lot of experience training the high-powered, beautiful Thoroughbreds at Whitebrook. Two years ago she had helped train March to Glory, getting him over his spooking and other problems on the track. Glory then set a world record for the mile and a quarter in the Breeders' Cup Classic and had been named Horse of the Year. Starting last fall, Cindy had trained Storm's Ransom from an unbroken colt to a gentlemanly, well-mannered horse who won two important sprints and a mile race this fall at Churchill Downs. She was determined to do the same now for Wonder's Champion.

"He's full of himself today," Ian remarked as Cindy stopped the colt in front of him.

"He always is." Cindy stretched forward to warm her fingers on Champion's chocolate-colored neck. But Cindy knew that when she rode Champion, she stayed cold only a few minutes, tops. The colt was always difficult to control, and Cindy was certain she would soon be struggling with him.

"Let's try an easy, long conditioning gallop today," Ashleigh said, her eyes narrowing with concentration. She was holding her daughter, Christina, who would be a year old on Christmas Day. Shortly after Christina's birth Ashleigh had resumed training and riding as a jockey for Whitebrook. She rode Mr. Wonderful, the three-year-old son of Ashleigh's

2

Wonder, Ashleigh's former miracle race mare, and also Storm for all their races.

Cindy had to smile at the well-bundled-up baby, snug in her pink snowsuit, with the hood tied tight around her small face as protection against the stinging air. Cindy could only see Christina's bright eyes, hazel just like Ashleigh's, and the tip of her nose. Cindy wondered if Christina loved being around horses as much as Ashleigh. The baby seemed to be watching with great interest the morning bustle of horses coming and going at the track.

"Don't let Champion work up any speed out there, Cindy," Ashleigh continued.

"I know he'll do better today," Cindy said quickly. But she remembered with frustration her ride on Wonder's Champion two days ago. The frisky colt had run away with her for almost a furlong during his morning exercise. Mike and Cindy's dad, Ian, had then replaced Cindy with Vic Teleski, one of Whitebrook's full-time grooms and exercise riders, for the rest of the exercise session. The consequences had been disastrous. The rambunctious colt had run away again, this time for two furlongs. Vic finally managed to slow him, but Champion finished up the ride with an explosive series of bucks, dumping Vic onto the soft dirt of the track.

"He sure is big," Mike said, studying the colt. "His muscle development is amazing for his age."

"Didn't you say he looks like Satin Romance, the

champion two-year-old last year?" Cindy asked eagerly.

"He doesn't look like him anymore." Ian frowned sadly. "Satin Romance is dead. He had to be put down a couple of weeks ago when he was diagnosed with equine infectious anemia."

Cindy stared at her dad in shock. "Why didn't you tell me?" she asked. Last spring and summer several cases of equine infectious anemia, or swamp fever, had been diagnosed in Kentucky. The viral disease, spread by insects, had no vaccine or cure. For months every time one of the horses had a runny nose or slight fever, Cindy had been terrified they had come down with the virus. Cindy knew that epidemics could sweep farms, killing most or all of the horses. Many years ago a virus had devastated Edgardale, Ashleigh's family's farm.

Satin Romance had been a beautiful, valuable horse, Cindy thought. If he could get equine infectious anemia, it could happen to any horse.

"We didn't want to tell you about Satin Romance because we knew you were so worried about the disease," Ian said. "We all were. But Satin Romance was one of the last cases to be reported in Kentucky this year."

Wonder's Champion jumped a little sideways beneath her. Cindy tightened her reins, glad for once that he was acting up and distracting her. "So you think the horses could still get sick?" she asked.

"They could, but it's unlikely," Ashleigh said

4

reassuringly. "The insects are gone, so the horses are safe for the winter. We'll just have to see if the disease resurfaces in the spring."

Cindy nodded, but the lump in her throat wouldn't go away. She ordered herself not to worry about the disease now. If she did, she would just go crazy. And she had enough to do, getting Wonder's Champion around the track without his acting up.

"I'll go with you," Ashleigh said. "Here comes Samantha—she's bringing Mr. Wonderful and Limitless Time."

Turning in the saddle, Cindy saw Samantha McLean, her nineteen-year-old sister, leading the two horses up from the training barn. Limitless Time was the yearling colt of Fleet Goddess, one of Ashleigh's former prize racemares. A bright bay with a beautiful head and a sweet disposition, he was a favorite to work with among the Whitebrook staff.

Mr. Wonderful, an elegant honey-colored chestnut, was walking quietly on the other side of Samantha. The colt had missed the Triple Crown races last spring due to a leg injury. He had come back in the fall of his three-year-old season, winning the Woodward at Belmont, but missed the Breeders' Cup when his injury flared up. Mr. Wonderful's injury had been a severe disappointment for Whitebrook, but now the colt was headed for big winter races in Florida, including the Donn Handicap at Gulfstream Park in mid-February.

Vic and Mark Collier, Whitebrook's other full-time

exercise rider, fought with each other for the privilege of riding Mr. Wonderful. Cindy knew that she was the only one who wanted to ride Wonder's Champion.

But Cindy loved the unruly colt. She had worked with him almost his whole life, watching him grow from a tiny foal into a perfectly correct yearling. Cindy was sure he had talent—if she could get through to him so that he could use it. She had ridden the colt for almost two months, and every exercise session had ended in near disaster. Wonder's Champion had tried every trick in the book—nipping other horses, running away with his rider, bucking. He was even difficult to saddle because he rarely stood still for more than a second.

"You'd better behave today," Cindy warned the colt. "Dad and Mike have had about enough of you."

Wonder's Champion suddenly stopped fidgeting, as if he understood her words. Cindy took advantage of his brief calm mood to lean back in the saddle and relax.

The sun, barely above the horizon, was a pink ball immersed in a cloud bank. Cindy loved the cold winter mornings out with the horses. The frigid blanket of stillness was broken only by the quick snorting breaths of the horses as they galloped around the track and the quiet comments of Ashleigh, Mike, and Ian to the riders.

"Hi, guys," Samantha said as she handed Mr. Wonderful's reins to Ashleigh and adjusted a helmet over her red hair. "Ready?" she asked with a smile.

Ashleigh mounted up on Mr. Wonderful. "Let's get out there!" she said.

Cindy was thrilled to hear Ashleigh's words. As many times as Cindy had ridden on the track, she never tired of the smooth feel of the reins in her hands as an eager Thoroughbred pulled on them, asking to run, and the rapid, rhythmic strides of the horse surging beneath her as they flew across the harrowed dirt of the track.

Cindy gave Wonder's Champion just a little rein, signaling him to trot. The dark brown colt promptly skittered sideways across the track.

"Look out!" Samantha cried.

Wonder's Champion bumped Limitless Time's hindquarters hard with his shoulder, almost knocking the colt into the rail. Limitless Time threw up his head and half reared.

"Champion, stop it!" Cindy pulled sharply on the colt's reins to straighten him.

"We're okay," Samantha called. Samantha had already gotten Limitless Time back under control and was heading the colt straight up the track.

With a sharp snort Wonder's Champion plunged after her. "You got away with bolting before, and you think you're going to again," Cindy said between gritted teeth as she hauled on the reins. "Well, you're not!"

The colt slowed to a slightly uneven trot, his long

legs effortlessly putting away ground on the backstretch. He eyed her backward with his large, prominent dark eyes. He seemed to know she meant business now, Cindy noted with relief.

"We'll gallop at the quarter pole, where we usually do," she told him. "I'd almost rather start back here, in case you throw a fit again. But Dad and Mike have to watch. Don't let me down, boy."

Around the far turn Cindy saw Ashleigh breezing Mr. Wonderful. The colt looked like a golden comet as he swept across the gray morning sky.

"Okay, Champion," Cindy said. Her heart pounded with anticipation as the quarter pole flashed by. She crouched forward, burying her hands deep in Wonder's Champion's thick brown mane. "Go!"

The magnificent colt didn't have to be asked twice. In an instant he had changed gear and was galloping smoothly, his hooves plunging into the dirt.

"Easy, boy!" Cindy called, checking him with her seat and hands. But she felt a rush of exhilaration at the young horse's driving speed.

This is so fantastic! Cindy exulted. *Instead of acting up, he's running his heart out!*

The colt's energetic buck caught her almost by surprise. "No, Champion!" Cindy cried as she gripped his mane, desperately trying to keep her seat in the small exercise saddle.

The colt roared ahead, flicking his tail and ignoring her. With a lurch Cindy righted herself in the saddle and pulled back on the reins, but she knew she was fighting a will as strong as her own. "I'm going with you, wherever we're going!" she said determinedly.

Wonder's Champion pounded into the stretch at a dead run. At the gap Cindy could see that Samantha and Ashleigh had stopped their horses. Samantha was urging Limitless Time off the track, out of the rampaging colt's way.

We may run into something! Cindy thought. She tried not to panic, but an icy chill of fear ran down her back. She wasn't afraid for herself but for the young horse with his sensitive bones, muscles, and tendons. *If only he gets tired of this before he gets hurt!*

At the gap Wonder's Champion abruptly slowed. "Good!" Cindy called tersely. She instantly took up on the reins and forced the colt to make a wide circle, bringing him down to a slow gallop, then a trot. When she had him completely under control, she aimed him back at the gap. Wonder's Champion whinnied a sprightly greeting to Mr. Wonderful, as if all along he had only intended to join the other horses.

Cindy dismounted and tucked the reins under her arm, flexing her fingers. They would hardly straighten from trying to hold back the strong colt. "I'm really sorry," she said unhappily to Ashleigh, Mike, and Ian. Cindy knew she was lucky the colt's escapade hadn't resulted in serious injury.

"Don't worry." Ashleigh touched her shoulder. "Champion goes better for you than anyone else,

Cindy," she said encouragingly. "He may just need to outgrow all those high jinks."

Champion edged closer and nibbled Cindy's shirt. *He looks pleased with himself*, Cindy thought. He certainly wasn't sorry that the exercise session had gone so badly.

"That's it for him." Ian shook his head. "I'm taking him out of training."

"No! It was my fault," Cindy said quickly. "I was just so excited because Champion did what he was supposed to for the first time."

"Yes, but if he'd gotten injured, it wouldn't have mattered how well he did," Ian said.

"We were going to take him out of training pretty soon for the winter anyway," Mike added. "He may be a different horse in the spring, like Ash said—when he grows up some more."

I sure hope so, Cindy thought. She wanted Mike and Ian to change their minds about taking Champion out of training, but she had to admit she agreed with them. The deep brown colt, with his rich, flowing mane and tail, bright blaze, and satin white stockings was one of the most gorgeous horses Cindy had ever seen, but for the first time she felt a flicker of fear that he really was untrainable.

"Here comes somebody you know, Cindy," Samantha said, pointing at the barns. Her tone was sympathetic.

Cindy glanced over her shoulder and her expression immediately brightened. "Storm!" she cried. Len, the farm manager, was leading the tall charcoal gray colt up to the track. Cindy's heart lifted as Storm's Ransom whinnied joyously at the sight of her.

"I'm glad to see you, too," Cindy said with a broad smile. *I'll focus on Storm for a while,* she thought. *He's been training perfectly, and everybody thinks he's got a great future.*

"I'll trade you Storm for Champion," Len said with a wink.

"Okay." Cindy grinned. "I'm not sure it's a fair trade, though."

Wonder's Champion nipped Cindy's sleeve affectionately as Len gathered his reins. The big chestnut colt seemed to be saying, No hard feelings.

Cindy patted his blaze. "I know you don't mean to be bad," she said. "But you've really got to shape up, Champion—like Storm. He always behaves himself." Storm was lovingly nuzzling her hands, tickling her with his warm, sweet-smelling breath and soft muzzle.

Champion snorted loudly, as if he resented the comparison. Cindy laughed and pressed her cheek against Storm's warm gray neck. Storm had always been the perfect gentleman, from the day Mike and Ian had bought him at the Keeneland select yearling sale over a year ago. His breeding had indicated he would be a superb sprinter, and so far he had been.

"Do you want me to take Storm around, Cindy?"

Ashleigh asked. "Have you had enough for today?"

"No, I'm all right," Cindy answered. She felt better just seeing the lovely dark gray colt. "I like to ride Storm," she added. "I always do."

Ashleigh smiled. "I know he wants you to ride him, too. Warm him up, then gallop him halfway around the track. I'll take him around once after that to get him ready for the race." In two days Ashleigh would be riding the colt at Churchill Downs in the Kentucky Jockey Club, a race at one and one-sixteenth miles. It would be Storm's first race at over a mile, and Cindy wondered how he would do. Not all sprinters could make the jump to longer races.

She pushed away her doubts. *Storm's going to circle the field*, she assured herself. Cindy quickly mounted up with a hand from her dad and settled into Storm's familiar saddle. She headed Storm around the track at a brisk walk.

The sun burst out of the cloud bank in a blaze of yellow beams, and the dust kicked up by Storm's hooves glittered in the sudden strong light. Giving his head a spirited toss, Storm moved out at an easy trot.

Cindy's heart filled with happiness and pride at the colt's willing sweetness. Storm loved to run, but he always obeyed her. He seemed to sense that they were a team. Cindy was proud of her training of the colt—her hard work with him over the past year had certainly paid off.

"I know you're going to run your best races yet," she murmured.

Cindy leaned over Storm's neck, letting his silken gray mane brush her face. Leaning forward was usually the request for speed, and Cindy knew that Champion would have roared out from under her like a shot. But Storm's strides stayed perfectly even as he huffed out quick breaths into the cold air.

"You're a wonderful boy," she said softly. "Do you know that?" Next to Glory, Cindy had never felt closer to a horse.

Storm's small, black-tipped ears flicked as he acknowledged her words. Smiling, Cindy sat back in the saddle and prepared herself mentally to gallop him at the half-mile marker. Storm was an easy horse to handle, but Cindy was always alert in her riding. Even a slight stumble or misstep could cause injury.

The marker pole loomed on the backstretch, and Cindy crouched over the colt's neck. "Now, boy!" she cried.

Taking a huge lunge, Storm shifted into a gallop in a bare stride. Cindy's heart hammered with excitement. The gray colt had so much early speed, the hallmark of a sprinter!

The first set of horses had left the track for the barn, and the other exercise riders were gathered around the gap, preparing to take out a group of two-year-olds. Cindy had the track to herself as Storm bounded around the far turn into the stretch, all power, beauty, and will to run. The fresh wind made Cindy's eyes tear and brought color to her cheeks, but she felt warm and happy.

"If only we could go on forever," she whispered to the flying colt. "But you have to race, Storm. You're going to be the fastest horse in the world."

2

LATER THAT MORNING CINDY RAN UP THE PATH FROM THE training barn to the smaller stallion barn. "Okay, I'm coming—don't break down the barn!" she called with a laugh to Glory. From the far end she could hear the big gray horse battering his stall door with an impatient hoof.

Whitebrook's six stallions—March to Glory, Wonder's Pride, Jazzman, Maxwell, Blues King, and Sadler's Station—were all looking out of their stalls, expecting breakfast. The horses in training had been fed earlier to ready them for their exercise.

Beautiful as all the stallions were, Cindy's eyes had gone quickly to the farthest stall, where Glory's elegant dapple gray head was over the stall door. A sharp whinny pierced the air as Cindy approached his stall. Glory, his large dark eyes bright with impatience and anticipation, leaned over the door as Cindy dug in her pocket for a carrot.

"Happy Thanksgiving to you, too," she said, stroking his black and gray mane.

Cindy stepped into the stall, running her hands over Glory's sleek neck and down his rippling shoulder muscles. She still couldn't quite get used to the fact that Glory was in the stallion barn, not the training barn, away from the exciting preparations for racing. Last year after his stunning Breeders' Cup victory in the Classic, Glory had raced twice, but then had to be retired after tendon trouble. Glory could be ridden as a pleasure horse, but he would never race again.

Glory had been a superhorse who had set a record in almost all his races, and Cindy had thrilled to see him run. *But he's still a superhorse to me,* she reminded herself. *And I love having him at home all the time.* If Glory's career had to end in injury, at least it was one he had recovered from, she thought. He was away from the excitement of the track—but also its dangers.

Cindy hugged her horse hard. "You've always been a fighter," she said quietly. She had ridden and trained Glory for over two years, since she had found him wandering in the woods, a runaway from cruel trainers. With Cindy's help, Glory had become a legendary champion of the stature of his grandsire, Just Victory.

Now everyone at Whitebrook hoped that Glory could pass on to his colts and fillies the heart, speed, and stamina of the Just Victory line. He would be bred for the first time this winter.

Glory whickered. His tone wasn't demanding, but Cindy understood. "I know, boy—you're hungry on these cold mornings," she said, heading to the feed room to get his grain. Cindy quickly filled Glory's bucket with his morning ration of oats.

On the way back down the aisle she touched Wonder's Pride's nose, and the chestnut stallion bobbed his head, grateful for the attention. Cindy thought with a little smile how different laid-back Wonder's Pride was from his bristly half brother, Wonder's Champion.

But that just makes Champion interesting to work with, she thought as she poured Glory's feed into his box. The big gray horse whickered throatily and dug in to his breakfast. *I really hope something changes by spring so that I can handle Champion better, though.*

"Let's get up to the house," Len suggested, walking up behind her. "I'm going to stop by my cottage and get cleaned up, then go to your folks' place."

"Okay." Cindy's parents were planning a big early dinner for Thanksgiving.

She jogged up the path to her family's small, cozy white cottage, tucked into a rise at the top of the hill. Whitebrook was a gracious two-hundred-year-old farm, and this morning the red-painted training, stallion, and mares' barns were coated with a light dusting of frost. The McLeans' cottage was next to Ashleigh and Mike's large house, which was part of the original old farm. Len's cottage was behind the barns.

Cindy thought the house and cottages were beautiful, but her favorite part of Whitebrook was the mile-long training track, where she exercised the horses every morning, and the paddocks and galloping lanes, surrounded by an almost endless line of white board fences. Cindy knew every inch of the track and lanes, where nearly every day she rode the quality Thoroughbreds that lived at Whitebrook.

Cindy felt proud that this was her home, and she never took it for granted. She had lived at Whitebrook for only two and a half years, after Ian and Beth McLean had adopted her, saving her from a bad foster home. Cindy couldn't imagine living anywhere else now. This was her home and family, and always would be.

Cindy opened the cottage door, and instantly the savory smells of turkey, dressing, and pumpkin pie enveloped her. She smiled, anticipating the feast that was to come.

In the hallway Cindy stepped carefully over a folded-up stroller, a Raggedy Ann, and a stuffed walrus and looked into the living room. *This house sure is different from the way it was a year ago*, she thought as the happy squeals of two babies greeted her. Cindy had a new little brother, Kevin McLean. He had been born in May and was six months old. Christina was also in the living room, trying to climb on a very small rocking horse.

Beth McLean poked her head out of the kitchen.

Cindy thought her mom looked stressed. In addition to doing child care Beth ran an aerobics business in Lexington.

"I'll watch the kids," Cindy volunteered quickly.

"Would you? That would be an enormous help." Beth pushed back a lock of her curly blond hair and wiped her forehead with the back of her hand. "Mike and Ian had them out at the barn, but they decided it was too cold."

"It's pretty nippy." Cindy hung up her coat and held out her arms to the two babies. "Come to Aunt Cindy!" she called.

Christina was already skimming along the furniture, trying to reach Cindy. Little red-haired Kevin could still only crawl. He looked a lot like his sister, Samantha, Cindy thought as the baby pounded his way along the floor. He already had a lot of determination.

In a few minutes Cindy was joined by Ashleigh, Mike, and Samantha. Ian, Len, and Beth finished preparing the dinner and finally brought in a large, delicious-looking turkey on a china platter.

Beth sat the two babies next to each other in high chairs. "I don't know how long this will last before they start screaming or throwing food at each other," she said with a laugh.

"They look adorable now," Samantha said.

"They sure do," Cindy agreed. She thought it was great that the two babies had come to the Whitebrook household.

"Let us give thanks," Ian said when they were all seated. "We have so very much to give thanks for this year. We have a new child, and all our children and our horses are happy and healthy."

Cindy bowed her head, giving special thanks that the viral epidemic had passed. Whitebrook had been so lucky that the horses were spared, she thought.

Mike cut thick slices of the succulent bird, golden brown and steaming on the platter. "Ian and Ashleigh, I just heard that Fanciful Dream has been scratched from the Kentucky Jockey Club," he said. "The colt's got filling in an ankle."

Cindy set down her fork, piled high with sweet potatoes. That was great news for Storm. Fanciful Dream had been the favorite going into the race, and Storm should have a much easier trip now. "Do you think Storm's going to win?" she asked.

"It's still guesswork," Ashleigh replied. "This is the first time we've tried him at a mile and a sixteenth. Storm won at a mile in the Iroquois this fall, but it was close. He may really have to put out an effort to win on Saturday."

"Storm is a sprinter by breeding," Ian said. "But we should certainly see what the colt is capable of. He may be able to go the distance."

"I bet he can," Cindy said confidently. Storm never gave less than a hundred percent at the track, she thought. She had never ridden a horse that tried harder at everything he did.

"I think so, too." Ashleigh smiled at her. "I'm looking forward to the race."

A little while later Cindy heard a knock on the door. "That's Heather," she said. Cindy had invited Heather Gilbert, her best friend, over for dessert. Cindy and Heather were both in eighth grade and shared a number of classes, but the main interest they had in common was horses.

Cindy opened the door. "Hi," Heather said with a smile.

"Hi, Heather. Come on in."

As they approached the table Kevin let out a wail. He was quickly joined by Christina.

"I think these little ones need naps," Ashleigh said. She took her small daughter out of the high chair and cuddled her.

"I'd best get back to the horses." Len stood up. "Many thanks for a delicious meal."

"You're most welcome, Len," Beth said warmly.

Within minutes the living room had cleared. "I guess it's just you and me, Heather," Cindy said, cutting two pieces of pumpkin pie.

"So how did Wonder's Champion do when you rode him this morning?" Heather asked.

Cindy shook her head. "Not well at all. He almost threw me, and Dad's taking him out of training."

"Oh no!" Heather looked shocked.

"It's not the end of the world, I guess," Cindy said. "They had planned to take him out of training

21

for the winter soon anyway. Dad, Mike, and Ashleigh think he'll go better when he grows up some more. But I'm not so sure. He'll be bigger and smarter—"

"But he's already too big and smart," Heather finished.

Cindy laughed. "Exactly. I'm going to keep trying with him," she said determinedly. "But in the meantime it's great that I have Storm. I really think this year he's going to be unbeatable."

"He sure looks good when you ride him," Heather agreed.

"Do you want to come to the race on Saturday?" Cindy asked.

"I wouldn't miss it." Heather's eyes sparkled. "With Storm running and Ashleigh riding, it's going to be a great show."

Cindy had expected that her friend would be eager to join her. Like Cindy, Heather loved horse events. Heather's own main focus was jumping. She took lessons once a week with Tor Nelson, Samantha's boyfriend, who with his father owned a jumping stable near Lexington. Tor was an excellent teacher and had helped Heather build up her confidence in jumping.

"It's good Ashleigh's riding Storm in the race," Cindy said, taking another bite of pie. "This is the first race he'll be going over a mile."

"I bet they can win," Heather said loyally.

"Yeah, it's good that the favorite in the race got

scratched. But I wish I could ride Storm." Cindy sighed, cupping her chin in her hand. She would turn fourteen in March, but she couldn't ride at the track until she was sixteen. "Ashleigh says Storm's a joy to ride in races."

"You can always ride Wonder's Champion when you're old enough," Heather reminded her.

Cindy groaned. "I don't know about that after this morning! I bet Dad is going to give me trouble about riding Champion in the spring because he's so dangerous." Cindy shook her head. "I'll be sixteen when he's four, and he'll probably still be racing. But right now it's kind of hard to imagine." Cindy frowned. She had been sure that Wonder's beautiful son would be a phenomenon at the track, maybe even Whitebrook's first Triple Crown winner. It had been so long since any horse won the Triple Crown.

Cindy hadn't given up her dreams for the colt completely. But after this morning, they didn't seem as real as they had.

"Do you think Mike and your dad will sell him?" Heather asked tentatively.

"No, not now—nobody thinks he's hopeless yet. I still think he's got a lot of talent," Cindy said, pushing back her blond hair. "I've got all winter to figure out how to handle him better the next time I ride."

Cindy reminded herself that there were usually setbacks and detours in training a horse. And she knew that she had to accept that some horses would never make it to the track at all.

But when I was training Storm, he was so different from Champion, Cindy thought. In fact, he was the easiest horse she'd ever trained. There had been no setbacks or detours with Storm. He had been nothing but pure, sweet willingness. After her morning run-in with Wonder's Champion, Cindy realized how rare that was. *I wonder if there's ever been a horse like Storm before?*

3

"HE LOOKS GOOD, DOESN'T HE, LEN?" CINDY ASKED AS she gave Storm's coat a final, firm rub with the finishing cloth and stepped back in the shedrow aisle to admire her work. The horses had just been called to the saddling paddock for the Kentucky Jockey Club at Churchill Downs that Saturday.

Storm's dark gray coat glittered like mica, and a thousand new sparkles flashed with the colt's every supple movement. Storm tucked his head around and fondly nuzzled Cindy.

"I've never seen him look better," Len agreed. "Well, let's head on out."

"Storm seems so relaxed," Heather said as they walked to the saddling paddock. Dozens of horses in racing sheets and tack followed their grooms and trainers to and from the barns and track. Whinnies of excited horses and the calls of grooms, trainers, and owners filled the crowded backside.

"Yeah, he always is. That's really unusual," Cindy said. Unlike almost every racehorse Cindy had ever known, Storm was always completely calm before his races. Maybe, she thought, it was because he saved all his energy for the race.

Cindy felt relaxed herself as she, Len, and Heather guided Storm to the saddling paddock. The weather was chilly but bright, and a clear blue sky outlined the graceful white buildings at the famous old Churchill Downs track.

This is definitely my favorite racetrack, Cindy thought. She had seen many big racetracks across the country, and most of them were beautiful or even lavish, but none of them could compare with Churchill Downs. Cindy had so many good memories of the track, and Whitebrook had so much history there. Glory had blazed to a win in an allowance race at Churchill Downs, and Wonder and Wonder's Pride had won the greatest prize in Thoroughbred racing there when they had run to Kentucky Derby victories.

And now Storm was at this track. Cindy smiled and rested her hand gently against the colt's sleek shoulder. Storm quickly swung his head around and whickered appreciatively.

"The track's fast," Len commented as he tightened the small racing saddle on Storm's back in the saddling paddock.

"That's good." Cindy nodded. Storm could run fairly well in mud, but it wasn't his favorite surface.

26

Cindy remembered fondly how Glory had sloshed happily through mud on the racetrack and on the trails at home. But most horses disliked the slap of mud in their face and had trouble handling the slippery surface.

Cindy watched closely as Len led Storm around the walking ring. She tried to gauge the competition as the colt circled in front of the onlookers. Storm was definitely the most beautiful horse in the field, but the others looked fit to race, too. Directly in front of Storm a groom was leading Just So Fleet, a West Coast horse who was a sprinter like Storm and running for the first time at a distance over seven furlongs. Just So Fleet was known for early speed, but Cindy knew it remained to be seen if the red chestnut colt could stay the distance.

"Which horse is that?" Heather asked, pointing to a lanky black across the ring. "He's so tall!"

"That's Forever Flush," Cindy replied, feeling nervous as the black colt closed the gap between himself and Storm. She knew that Storm would never act unmannerly in the walking ring, but Forever Flush had a reputation for it. Storm had raced against Forever Flush in the Iroquois three weeks ago, and the other colt had kicked a groom in the walking ring and almost thrown his jockey in the gate. "He'll be a contender if his jockey can control him," Cindy added. "He only came in third in the Iroquois because he broke badly from the gate, but he had a real closing kick. This race is a mile and one-sixteenth, so he might have time to close."

"Not while Storm's racing," Heather said with conviction. Storm was eagerly walking, dancing a little sideways. His eyes were bright with anticipation and his ears were pricked.

"I don't think so either." Cindy shared the colt's excitement about the upcoming race. The competition was stiff, even though Fanciful Dream had been scratched, but Cindy was confident Storm could handle it.

Checkpoint Lady and Sadie's Soldier, two Florida-breds, headed for the track with their jockeys up. It was almost race time.

"I'm ready," Ashleigh said as she, Mike, and Ian joined Cindy, Len, and Heather in the walking ring. Ashleigh wore the sky-blue-and-white racing silks of Whitebrook. *She looks so pretty and professional*, Cindy thought admiringly. Mike gave Ashleigh a leg into the saddle.

"You know we're going to have to play things a little differently in this longer race," Ian cautioned Ashleigh. "Probably Storm will want to lead wire to wire. That's what he's done in sprints, and he got away with it in the Iroquois. But I don't know if that will work in a longer race—he may come up empty in the stretch and get caught by a closer."

Ashleigh nodded. "I'll try to rate him. I don't want him to be surprised by the extra distance." She brushed Storm's thick mane lightly with her hand. "Time to get out there!"

"Good luck, Ashleigh." Cindy smiled up at her. "Go for it, boy," she added to Storm.

Storm sniffed her hands deeply, as if he were memorizing her scent. Then he turned abruptly to follow the other horses toward the track.

"I wish I could tell Ashleigh to be careful out there," Mike said. "I'm much more worried about her riding now that we've got Christina."

"Ashleigh's one of the top jockeys in the world, Mike, as you well know," Ian said comfortingly. "If anyone can stay out of trouble, it's Ashleigh."

"I wonder if anyone will ever say that about me?" Cindy whispered to Heather as they walked to their seats. "You know, that I'm one of the top jockeys in the world."

"I think you'd have to win a horse race first." Heather giggled.

"Thanks a lot," Cindy said. She glanced at the odds board. She felt a surge of pride when she saw that Storm was going into the race as the favorite. *I'd like to tell everybody here that I helped to train that horse,* she thought.

Beth and Samantha were already sitting in the stands. "How's Storm?" Samantha asked.

"Acting like a pro," Mike said with a smile.

Cindy sat in between Mike and Heather and looked quickly out at the track to see if Storm had stayed calm. The tall gray colt seemed perfectly collected as he paced by the stands in the post parade with the other eight horses in the field. All the horses stepped easily in the gate behind an attendant. Storm had loaded into the number-four slot.

"Forever Flush usually causes problems in the gate. But he's behaving himself today," Ian commented.

Cindy nodded. For a second she almost wished Forever Flush would lose his concentration in the gate. Storm's race would be easier—the black colt was his greatest threat. Then she reminded herself not to be so competitive. *If Forever Flush had acted up in the gate, he might have hurt himself or his jockey*, she thought. *I sure don't want Storm to win because of that.*

"The horses are in the gate," the announcer called. The bell clanged loudly and the doors flipped open. "They're off!"

Cindy half rose from her seat, trying to see Storm's position in the fast-moving pack. "Is he on the lead?" she asked anxiously.

"I don't think so!" Heather sounded as worried as Cindy.

"He's in fifth," Ian said with a frown.

Cindy stared out at the track, her forehead creased with worry. Storm had never been that far back in a race! "What's wrong?" she asked with a sinking heart. Now she could see Storm rapidly galloping just behind the frontrunners. The colt seemed to be moving well, but he was dropping even farther back.

"He got pushed back after the break," Mike

answered over the cheers of the spectators. "I don't think Ashleigh's rating him."

"Storm may be in just the right place." Samantha's binoculars were glued to the track. "Look at the board—the field set very fast fractions for the first half mile. He'll have something left."

"He's not used to running off the pace." Mike shook his head. "We'll just have to see if he fires at some point."

"And it's Forever Flush on the lead; two lengths back to Checkpoint Lady," called the announcer. "Sadie's Soldier and Just So Fleet are neck and neck for third, followed by Storm's Ransom. . . ."

The horses swept into the backstretch. Now Cindy could clearly see Storm. The dark gray colt was running behind Checkpoint Lady, Sadie's Soldier, and Just So Fleet, who were blocking Storm's path. Storm's strides looked strong and even to Cindy, and he didn't seem to be laboring. *He's still in striking position,* Cindy thought, drawing a deep breath.

In a split second Forever Flush slowed and dropped back. "His jockey's pulling him up!" Cindy cried. The black colt fell back to last and finally broke into a trot as his jockey guided him to the outside of the track.

"That's a lucky break for us," Mike said.

"I just hope he's not seriously hurt." Beth shook her head.

"Me too," Cindy agreed. She clenched her jaw. Even with Forever Flush out of the race, Storm was barely holding his position in fourth. *This distance and pace may just be too much for him*, Cindy thought worriedly. The horses roared into the stretch with Storm still in fourth.

"They're headed for home," the announcer called.

"Storm has to make his move or he's never going to get up in time!" Cindy cried.

"I think he will." Ian reached across Mike to pat her hand.

Cindy saw that Sadie's Soldier was beginning to tire. The bay colt faded to third, then fifth. But Checkpoint Lady and Just So Fleet, running close together ahead of Storm, still blocked Storm's path.

"He doesn't have time to go around them, does he?" Heather asked.

"I don't think so." Cindy shook her head in despair.

"Look! Just So Fleet is bearing out—there goes Storm between horses!" Samantha cried. Suddenly Storm was closing fast. He roared through the hole between Checkpoint Lady and Just So Fleet.

"He's got room! Yes! Run them down, boy!" Cindy jumped to her feet, punching the air.

"And Storm's Ransom is making his move!" the announcer called. "He's up with Just So Fleet and Checkpoint Lady—he's ahead by a neck!"

"Careful, Ashleigh—don't interfere with them!" Mike cried. Cindy knew that if Ashleigh and Storm bumped other horses in the race or interfered with

32

them in any other way, the racetrack officials would move them out of first place.

"She didn't bump them!" Cindy was squeezing her hands in delight. "Storm's a length ahead!"

The gray colt was unstoppable. Tail and mane blowing as he fully extended his stride, he was exquisitely beautiful. Like a fast-moving storm cloud on the horizon, he flew under the wire.

"And it's Storm's Ransom, with Ashleigh Griffen up for the win!" the announcer cried.

"Come on, everybody." Ian was all smiles. "Let's get down to the winner's circle!"

"I can hardly believe it." Cindy hugged Heather and Samantha.

Posting lightly, Ashleigh rode Storm across the track to greet them in front of the winner's circle. "That was close for a few seconds there," she said with a grin.

"You pulled it off," Mike replied.

"You sure did—great ride, Ashleigh!" Cindy said happily. She went immediately to Storm's head. "And you were just fantastic, boy!"

The gray colt rubbed his head hard on her shirt and shook himself from head to tail, scattering drops of sweat. *He's soaked!* Cindy thought with alarm. Storm dropped his wet head into her arms and huffed out a sigh. Then he jerked his head away again. He was still wired from his effort.

"I'm amazed he was able to change his running style like that," Mike shouted over the cheers and calls of the crowd.

"So was I." Ashleigh dismounted, then immediately looked over Storm. Cindy knew that Ashleigh's practiced eye was instantly taking in the colt's condition. "One quick picture, then let's get him back to the barn," she said. Ashleigh took the saddle to weigh in.

Storm bobbed at the end of the reins, dancing in place. Cindy felt her initial scare about his condition fading. Storm was tired, but obviously he felt great. "You know just how well you did," she said, rubbing his damp neck.

"I'm glad I saw the race." Heather patted Storm, too.

"Well, it looks like Excellent Prize might have his first runner that can go the distance," one of the reporters commented. Cindy knew they were talking about Storm's sire.

"I wouldn't say that just yet." Mike shook his head. "But we're certainly happy and optimistic at this point."

After the winner's photograph was taken, Cindy led Storm to the backside to cool him out. Much as she thrilled to the praise of her horse, she was anxious to get him back to the barn and take care of him. The run had taken so much out of him.

In the barn Cindy ran a warm, soothing sponge over the colt's hot back. Storm grunted with pleasure and shivered. Cindy smiled. She loved the quiet time in the barn with him after a race. "I'm so proud of you, boy," she said. "I've never seen a horse try so hard."

"Is he okay?" Heather asked anxiously as Cindy led Storm out of the barn to walk him.

"Yeah, I think so." Cindy stopped Storm and carefully looked him over again. She was glad that the track required horses to be tested for equine infectious anemia before they raced, because one of its symptoms was fatigue. Remote as the chances were of Storm's having the disease, Cindy would have worried. Luckily Storm's test results had been negative. "We'll have to see if he eats and how his legs are tomorrow," she added to Heather. "But I know he feels good about winning."

When she was sure Storm was completely cooled down, Cindy brought him back into the barn and put him in his stall. She checked his water bucket and fluffed up the straw, then sat down with her back against the wall. Storm stretched his neck to nudge her knees.

"I guess this is where the party is," Heather said with a laugh as she joined them in the stall.

Cindy heard the swift tap of boots in the aisle, and a moment later Ashleigh looked over the stall door. "How's he doing?" she asked. Storm walked over to the door to greet his visitor.

"He seems fine now." Cindy lovingly ran her hand through Storm's silver tail. "But he seemed pretty tired after the race."

"Yes, I noticed." Ashleigh frowned and stepped into the stall. Cindy watched as Ashleigh slowly ran her hands up and down the colt's legs. "I don't find any heat or swelling," she said. "I think he handled the race just fine."

"Will he be running in distance races from now on?" Cindy asked. She felt a twinge of worry.

"We'll see." Ashleigh looked thoughtful. "We'd certainly want to consider it after today. But I do intend to be cautious, Cindy. Storm ran a great race, but he had a couple of lucky breaks. If Forever Flush hadn't quit, Storm might have been outrun. And if Just So Fleet hadn't drifted out, Storm could have been trapped. I don't think he could have powered around him for the win."

"So you don't think Storm can go the distance." Cindy frowned.

"He did today," Ashleigh said reassuringly. "Those things happen in almost every race. That Storm prevailed is what's important."

"It was a pretty amazing run," Cindy said. She stood up and stroked Storm's soft neck. The colt leaned into the caress, half closing his eyes as he relaxed into her arms.

"Storm was smart enough to change his running style and come from behind," Ashleigh said. "Of course we'll give him a good rest and keep evaluating him—we won't run him unless he's completely fit. But we want to give him a chance to show his true potential."

"When do you think he'll race again?" Cindy asked. She hoped Storm would have a long time to rest up.

"Not until at least January," Ashleigh said. "We'll probably take him to Gulfstream in Miami then."

Cindy hugged Storm tight. *I'm going to help you all I can so that you recover completely for the race*, she vowed. After a performance like today's, when the colt had shown so much courage, Cindy knew he deserved all the love and attention she could give him.

4

ON WEDNESDAY, CINDY SET HER BOOKS ON THE CAFETERIA table at school that she always shared with Heather and her other friends. Last year several other kids who were interested in horses had started sitting with Cindy and Heather at lunch to share horse stories.

Cindy opened her lunch bag, hoping that her mom, not her dad, had put together her lunch. Beth always carefully packed a nutritious, tasty meal, whereas Ian favored peanut butter sandwiches or crackers. Cindy knew she should make her lunch herself or not complain, but getting together a lunch would take away time from the horses in the morning. Cindy smiled when she saw the thick, luscious-looking turkey-and-avocado sandwich on wheat bread, Beth's trademark.

"Hi, Cindy." Melissa Souter sat down across from her, brushing back her long, light brown hair. "Hey, guess what the big news is today? My parents are sending three of our horses to Whitebrook for your dad to train."

"He told me. I helped to get the stalls ready yesterday," Cindy said, biting into her sandwich.

"Ready for what?" Max Smith asked as he sat next to Cindy. Max's mother was Whitebrook's veterinarian, and Max was one of Cindy's closest friends. In addition to her veterinary practice Dr. Smith reconditioned Thoroughbreds and quarter horses from the racetracks, turning them into pleasure horses and barrel racers.

Melissa explained to Max about the horses as Heather, Laura Billings, and Sharon Rodgers joined them at the table.

"Cool," Max said when Melissa had finished. "Can we see those horses sometime, Cindy?"

"Do you all want to come over today after school?" Cindy asked. "We can check out the Souters' horses and then ride some of ours. I'll call home and see if it's okay, and then you could all take the bus with me."

In history, her first class after lunch, Cindy had to force herself to listen to Mrs. Robbins's lecture. She had called home and gotten permission to bring her friends with her after school. Cindy's thoughts kept straying to the new horses at Whitebrook and the ride she had planned. *Pay attention,* she ordered herself. She had to do well in school. Ian and Beth had said that if Cindy's grades were satisfactory, she could miss some school this winter to be at the races with

Storm and Mr. Wonderful. *I absolutely don't want to mess that up*, she thought, focusing intently on Mrs. Robbins's lecture.

"Before we ride, can we look at your other horses?" Melissa asked that afternoon. Cindy and her friends were walking up the drive to Whitebrook from the bus.

"Sure," Cindy said. "We can start with the mares." She pointed to a big white-fenced paddock to the right of the drive. "Two of our best horses are in there—Ashleigh's Wonder and Shining."

Both mares were already on their way to the fence to greet the visitors. Cindy smiled at the expression in their intelligent, wide-set dark eyes. Treated gently and lovingly by Ashleigh and Samantha, Wonder and Shining liked people. Last year Shining had run a brilliant race in the Breeders' Cup Distaff. Now five, she was retired and expecting her first foal in the spring. Shining was in foal to Chance Remark, last year's winner of the Belmont Stakes.

Last spring Wonder had been bred again to Townsend Victor, Wonder's Champion's sire, but nothing had come of the mating. Wonder had always been tricky to breed, Cindy knew. *Champion is enough for us to handle now anyway*, she thought wryly. *A full brother or sister to Champion might be just like him.*

The dark chestnut colt was by himself in a paddock next to the mares. He had been put in

40

isolation since he kicked one of the other yearlings yesterday after a game had gotten too rough.

"You have so many wonderful horses," Melissa said enviously as she scratched Wonder's ears. "My dad wants to know how you guys do it."

"Ashleigh, Mike, and my dad all have a great eye for horses, I guess," Cindy said. "Wonder sure proves that. She was born small and weak. Only Ashleigh ever thought she'd make it as a racehorse, and for a while hardly anyone thought she would even live. And Mike picked Shining up at an auction for almost nothing. She was half starved, but he knew from her conformation and bloodlines—she's Wonder's half sister—that she could really be something. Then Wonder turned out to be as great a broodmare as she was a racehorse. She had Wonder's Pride and Townsend Princess, and now Mr. Wonderful is burning up the track."

"And you're working with Wonder's Champion," Heather said.

"I was." Cindy frowned, remembering her problems with the saucy colt.

Cindy heard a horse's sharp whistle. Looking over, she saw Glory out in one of the stallion paddocks. Glory was energetically pacing the fence line. Clearly he had no intention of being ignored. "I'll be right back," she told her friends. "I need to talk to Glory for a minute."

"I'll come with you," Max said. Cindy knew that the big gray horse was also a favorite of Max's. Max

41

had helped her protect Glory during Glory's racing days when a trainer had given him drugs to make him lose races. Cindy's close friendship with Max dated from then.

Glory whickered joyously at their approach. "Yes, you don't get all the attention now that you aren't racing, and you don't like it," Cindy said, standing on the lowest board of the fence. She rubbed the black tip of Glory's muzzle. "I'll take you out soon. But today I have to ride Storm." Cindy was still concerned about how Storm had come out of the race on Saturday. He wasn't eating well, and he had lost weight.

"Ouch!" Melissa cried.

Cindy spun around just in time to see Wonder's Champion backing away with a bit of Melissa's jacket in his teeth. "Champion!" Cindy shouted, running toward the paddock. The other kids laughed.

The chestnut colt gave a snort of alarm and galloped off, waving his tail high above his back. Cindy threw a handful of dry grass after him in frustration.

"Are you okay?" she asked Melissa with concern. Horses didn't have sharp teeth, but they could bite hard.

"I'm all right, but my jacket isn't," Melissa said ruefully, examining the rip. "That nasty guy."

"He isn't really." Cindy didn't know how to explain why Wonder's Champion acted the way he did sometimes. "He's just pesky," she said. "He likes to make trouble."

"Well, I'm staying away from him," Melissa said firmly. "I'd rather spend time with nicer horses."

Sometimes I feel that way too, Cindy thought with a sigh. "I'm sorry about your jacket," she said.

"Oh, it's okay." Melissa shrugged.

Cindy looked back as she and her friends walked away from the paddock. Champion stood at the gate, watching her wistfully. He seemed to be sorry that he'd driven everyone away. Cindy felt bad for him.

"I'll come see you later, boy," she called. Even though the colt was out of training, she was sure she needed to keep handling him. Cindy knew that Mike, Ashleigh, and Ian hoped the colt would do better in the spring, but Cindy wondered if they should have kept on with his training for another session or two. Somehow she was sure the intelligent colt would remember that last training session—and how he'd gotten his way.

"Where are our horses?" Melissa asked.

"I think Dad's keeping them in the barn today," Cindy answered. "He'll put them out in the paddock tomorrow."

In the training barn Cindy went right to the Souters' horses, which were stabled in a row. Two grays and a chestnut thrust soft muzzles over the stall door, asking to be petted.

"This guy's had foot trouble," Melissa said, rubbing the chestnut's forehead. "My parents are hoping your dad can bring him back into training without starting it up again."

"My dad's the best," Cindy assured her, going to

Storm's stall. The charcoal-colored colt had his head over the stall door and was watching Cindy and the new horses with interest.

"Are you going to ride Storm?" Heather asked.

"Sure. A little exercise would probably be good for him," Cindy replied. "I just need to double-check with Ashleigh that it's okay."

"We'll go with you," Sharon said eagerly.

Cindy smiled as her friends crowded around her in the doorway of the stable office. She realized that they wanted to see and meet Ashleigh almost as much as they'd wanted to visit the horses. Young as she was, Ashleigh was a legend as a jockey and trainer.

Ashleigh was sitting in front of a computer, examining pedigree records. Cindy introduced Sharon, Laura, and Melissa, who hadn't met Ashleigh before.

"Sure, it'd be good for Storm to get out," Ashleigh said when she heard Cindy's plan. "Just take it easy with him. He's not quite up to form."

"I know—I'll be careful," Cindy said eagerly.

Soon the barn rang with the excited voices of Cindy's five friends as they collected riding horses from the stalls Len pointed out. All six of the crossties in the barn were filled with horses as Cindy, Max, Sharon, Laura, Heather, and Melissa groomed and tacked them each up. Cindy smiled at the hubbub as she readied Storm for the outing. She enjoyed riding by herself, but it was fun to have company, too.

Cindy carefully checked Storm over. "You really have lost weight," she said, frowning. "You've got to eat and keep up your strength." Storm watched her backward with a calm brown eye as she ran a brush over his flank. Len had said that the colt still seemed wired from the race four days ago. *Well, he certainly doesn't seem wired now,* she thought.

"We're ready," Laura said, leading Chips toward the barn door. Chips was a trustworthy Appaloosa, and Cindy had selected the gelding for Laura since she was the least experienced rider of the group. Max followed with Ruling Spirit, the retired Thoroughbred racehorse that he usually rode at Whitebrook.

"Where do you want to ride?" Heather asked, shortening her reins on Bo Jangles. The almost black gelding was a favorite of hers.

"Why don't we just go around the training track?" Cindy suggested, joining her friends outside the barn. She lightly mounted up on Storm with a hand from Len. "We don't have time to do much more before it gets dark."

"Sounds great," Laura said eagerly.

Cindy frowned as she looked at the sky. A curtain of translucent, sheer gray clouds was moving in from the west. She knew that snow was expected. Snow seriously interfered with any training efforts.

Oh, well, she thought as she guided Storm to the training track. *At least we'll get in a ride now.*

On the track Cindy sat back in the saddle, enjoying the easy feel of Storm's fluid walk. She circled the track, then caught up to Max and Ruling Spirit on the backstretch.

After a few minutes Cindy and Max were joined by their other four friends and their horses. Six across, they trotted along the track, the horses' hooves churning the soft dirt.

Sharon leaned back in the saddle to look around Heather, who was riding Bo Jangles next to Cindy. "Should we race?" Sharon joked.

"Don't even think about it," Cindy warned. "Storm's the only racehorse out here, and I'm not planning to run him."

"I wish you could." Laura glanced over at Storm. "Isn't he incredibly fast?"

"He sure is." Cindy lovingly ran her hand along Storm's mane.

"How is Storm doing?" Heather asked. "He was so tired after the race."

"He's not a hundred percent yet." Cindy's smile slipped a little. "I hope getting out like this will give him an appetite. I should really ride him or walk him every day. I'm going to do everything I can to get him as fit as possible for his next race in January."

Cindy confidently patted Storm's neck. *It might be a lot of work to bring him back to top condition. But I'll do whatever it takes*, she thought.

Blizzards hit Whitebrook again and again over the next two weeks. Despite the snow, slush, and freezing rain, Cindy took Storm for a long, slow ride almost every day. When it was too icy to ride, she walked Storm on foot. Heather often accompanied her, leading Glory.

On Sunday it snowed, and Cindy fretted because she couldn't take Storm out at all. But the next day the blizzard passed, leaving glistening mounds of ice along the plowed roads and snow piled high in the trees. Right after school Cindy got Storm out of his stall for his exercise.

"Do you think this is getting Storm in shape?" Heather asked as she walked Glory with Cindy and Storm down a snowy lane. The snow had melted on top during the early afternoon but had refrozen and crunched under their feet. "I mean, I always love being with the horses, but it's kind of cold."

"I think Storm's almost in top shape." Cindy doggedly led the colt around a dead, snow-piled tree blocking the lane. Storm didn't seem to mind the weather at all, even when a weighted branch dropped a load of snow on his dark gray back. "Ashleigh used to walk Wonder when it was too icy to ride so Wonder wouldn't lose her conditioning," she added. "That's what gave me the idea. And it's working—Storm's been eating more. I think he could run in a sprint now if he had to. I don't know about another distance race, though."

"That's good." Heather rested her mittened hand against Glory's neck. Glory jumped lightly over a twig and skittered away from a flock of sparrows. He seemed to be saying that the quiet life of a retired racehorse didn't suit him at all.

Cindy smiled at him. *This really is fun*, she told herself. It was so hard walking through the snow that she didn't feel cold. And Storm had definitely brightened from the daily attention. His ears were flicking with interest at the soft thuds as more snow fell off the trees, and occasionally he leaned over to nudge Cindy gently with his muzzle.

They walked about a mile along the lane and into the woods. The cold winter sun had set, sending brilliant fingers of crimson and orange into the sky. The twilight was deepening around them.

"Don't you think we should go back?" Heather asked.

"Yeah, I guess so." Cindy glanced around. "It's getting dark."

Heather shivered. "It's kind of creepy out here."

Cindy glanced at the dark shapes of the trees, blackening as violet night spread over the sky. Then she looked back at Storm. Storm's ears were relaxed and he was walking very close to Cindy. *He would smell or hear if anything was threatening us*, Cindy thought. *I could just jump on his back and gallop away from danger. Nothing would be able to catch a horse as fast as Storm.*

"I'm not scared," Cindy said to Heather. "Storm will take care of me." The gray colt rested his head on her shoulder for a moment, as if to say she could count on it.

* * *

"Hey, Dad." Cindy waved at her father later that evening as she walked Storm down the barn aisle, followed by Heather. Storm's shod hooves clattered on the concrete aisle as he moved quickly in the direction of his stall, anticipating dinner. Heather had already put up Glory in the stallion barn.

"Hi, sweetie," Ian said. He set down a feed bucket and stood to the side of the aisle to let Cindy and Storm pass. "You two look frozen solid."

"We're not, though." Cindy brushed wisps of blond hair off her face.

"I'm fine," Heather agreed.

"So is Storm." Ian smiled. "This afternoon I entered him in his next race—the Holy Bull Stakes at Gulfstream, on January 20. That gives us over a month to get him ready."

Cindy stopped Storm in front of his stall and turned to her dad with a big smile. This was great news that Storm would be racing again! "I can go to the race, can't I?" Cindy asked eagerly.

Storm gently pawed the aisle, reminding her that it was time for him to eat. But it seemed to Cindy that he was anxious to be off to the races, too.

"Your grades are excellent—I don't see why not." Ian nodded.

"How long a race is the Holy Bull?" Cindy called over her shoulder as she let Storm into his stall.

"A mile and a sixteenth," Ian replied.

"Another distance race!" Cindy exclaimed. She

and Heather exchanged dismayed glances. Cindy wasn't really surprised that her dad had entered Storm in another long race—Storm had won his last race at a mile and a sixteenth. But it had taken her so long to get him over the effects of that race. Feeling uneasy, Cindy remembered how tired and thin Storm had been.

"We'll try it just one more time, and if it doesn't work, we'll put him back in sprints, Cindy," Ian said. "But I don't want to hold him back."

"Yes, I know," Cindy said hesitantly. She unclipped Storm's lead line in his stall, and the colt walked to his feed tray with a sprightly step.

"You don't think it's a good idea for him to run in that race, do you?" Heather whispered.

"Maybe it will be okay." Cindy rested her hand on Storm's flank. The gray colt was eating his dinner with gusto—his appetite was back. "I can see why Dad wants to run Storm in the Holy Bull," she said. "But I'm just not sure it will be good for him."

5

CINDY SURVEYED WITH SATISFACTION THE PILES OF brightly wrapped Christmas presents under the tree. She was the first up on Christmas morning, and the living room was utterly still. Dawn was approaching, but the house was still wrapped in thick silence.

Cindy flicked on the Christmas lights on the tree and shivered with delight, relishing the warm glow of the bulbs on the shiny, colorful packages.

"I *think* I got everybody something they'll like," she murmured to herself.

She sat cross-legged on the floor next to the tree and picked up the nearest present. It was wrapped in silver paper decorated with gold jumping horses, and the tag said it was for her. Cindy gave the package an experimental shake, then looked at the tag of the present under it. "All of these are for me?" she whispered, looking at more tags. Cindy had been raised an orphan after her parents had been killed in a car accident when she was a baby. She still never took lots of presents or happy Christmases for granted.

"Hey, Santa Claus," Samantha said with a laugh. Cindy looked up to see her older sister coming down the stairs in her pajamas, combing her red hair with her fingers.

"I'm just one of his elves." Cindy grinned.

As the day brightened, the rest of the household came downstairs. "I'll make coffee," Ian said, walking into the kitchen. Beth put down Kevin, who immediately crawled to the packages and began pulling off the bows.

When Ian returned with mugs of coffee for the adults and a cup of hot chocolate for Cindy, they began opening presents. Cindy watched anxiously to see if her family liked what she had gotten them.

"This tie is beautiful, Cindy," Ian said, lifting a green silk tie out of a small, flat box.

"I'm glad you think so," Cindy said shyly. She knew that buying a tie for her dad was kind of boring, but Ian always needed ties to wear on race days.

"Let's give Kevin his present from you and me before he tears up the rest of ours," Samantha said to Cindy. Cindy had split the cost with Samantha on a walker with wheels for Kevin.

They tore open the silver paper and placed Kevin in the walker. The baby crowed with pleasure but seemed content just to sit in the walker, watching the activity around him.

Cindy opened a box of clothes from a specialty horse-wear catalog. "Wow, look at these!" she said, holding up several pairs of riding jeans in beige, overdyed black, and stonewashed blue. She had also gotten a sweater with a hunt scene design.

Samantha held up a tiny silver-plated halter. "This is just what I wanted for Shining's foal," she said with a broad smile. "It's from Tor."

"I got a pesto grinder from Cindy!" Beth lifted the small stone device out of bright green tissue paper. "Well, I know what I'm going to be doing in the near future, since this is the third kitchen toy I've gotten," Beth said with a laugh. "Cooking!"

Cindy was intrigued by a long, flat box with her name on it. It was wrapped in blue and white paper—Whitebrook's racing colors.

"Why don't you open that one, Cindy?" Ian asked, smiling as he followed her gaze. "I think you'll like it."

Cindy carefully pulled off the tape and opened the wrapping paper. "Oh, my gosh!" Slowly she lifted a blue and white saddlecloth out of the box. "Storm's Ransom," she read aloud from the side of the saddlecloth. For her twelfth birthday Cindy's family had given her a similar saddlecloth for Glory. Now that he was retired from racing, she had hung it on the wall in her room.

Cindy held the saddlecloth to her cheek, unable to speak. The saddlecloth meant to her that the horse she had trained and loved was a special star in everyone's minds, just the way Glory had been. The card said that the saddlecloth was from her whole family. "Thanks, everyone," she finally managed to say. "This is the greatest present!"

"You're very welcome." Samantha smiled. "I think Storm's going to get a lot of use out of it."

"I know he will," Cindy said confidently.

"Let's head over to the Reeses' soon." Beth stood and picked Kevin up out of the walker. "We can exchange presents with them and start preparing Christmas dinner."

Cindy looked out the window. "There's still a foot of snow everywhere. I guess we can't ride today," she said with disappointment.

Beth dressed Kevin in his snowsuit, and they all put on heavy coats. Single file, the McLeans walked along the narrow cleared part of the path to the Reeses' farmhouse. Cindy brought up the rear, kicking up a spray of snow with her boot. The gray, leaden sky hugged the horizon, promising more snow. *I want to ride, but I guess today's a good day to be inside and enjoy my Christmas presents,* she thought.

"Come in," Ashleigh greeted them at the door. "Merry Christmas, everybody!"

"The same to you," Ian said as he stepped inside. "How are you, Gene?" Mr. Reese, Mike's father, was home from the hospital just for Christmas Day. He had been very ill with cancer for a long time.

"Just fine," Mr. Reese said. Christina was on the floor, playing with the wrapping paper.

"Excuse the mess." Ashleigh shook her head. "Our little terror has been at work."

"Come to Granddad," Mr. Reese said to Christina, opening his arms.

Christina opened her arms, too, then cruised to him, holding on to the furniture. Mr. Reese scooped her up and pressed his cheek to hers. Cindy saw that Mike's eyes were filled with tears. She knew that Mr. Reese wasn't expected to live much longer.

"I think this is the best Christmas we've ever had," Mr. Reese said contentedly, bouncing Christina on his knee.

"I'll take this Christmas over last year's, since I almost died in labor." Ashleigh looked thoughtful. "But in a way that was the best day of my life. After all, that was when Christina came into the world."

"Everything seems to have worked out for the best," Mike agreed, squeezing Ashleigh's shoulder. He and Ashleigh smiled at each other for a long moment. "I'm going to check on the horses—who's coming with me?" Mike added.

"I am." Cindy jumped up. "We have to wish them a merry Christmas! Come on, Christina," she said to the baby. "I'll give you a Christmas ride."

"Be careful." Beth looked uncertain.

"Oh, I will be," Cindy said reassuringly. "I'll take Christina around on Shining—Samantha said it's okay."

Samantha nodded. "Shining will like the attention."

Cindy picked up Christina. "Then I want to walk Storm and some of the other horses since we can't ride."

"That's a good idea," Mike said. "I just heard that Alyba, last year's champion two-year-old, will be running in the Holy Bull Stakes with Storm. Storm will have to be at the top of his game to take on a horse like that."

Cindy frowned. Alyba was probably headed for the Kentucky Derby in May, and so were some of the other horses in the Holy Bull. She knew Storm couldn't have tougher competition. *I'll take him for a really long walk today*, she decided.

"I'll get Christina ready and go down to the stables with you, Cindy," Ashleigh said.

The mares' barn was warm and peaceful, smelling sweetly of hay and horses. Cindy went straight to Shining's stall, and the roan mare whickered a friendly greeting. "Do you want to get out for a little while, girl?" Cindy asked. Shining's foal was due in April, so she could still move around well.

Cindy expertly brushed and tacked up the mare, then led her out into the stable yard. Samantha perched Christina on Shining's back and supported her.

Cindy carefully guided Shining around the stable yard, scuffing through the slushy melting snow. Shining seemed to be watching her step, too. "It's so funny that Shining is the perfect kids' horse," Cindy said to Samantha. "Most racehorses are so wired."

Shining was the first Thoroughbred Cindy had ever ridden.

"I think Shining really likes kids," Samantha replied.

Christina squealed with delight, patting Shining's neck with both hands. "And vice versa," Cindy said with a grin.

After about fifteen minutes Ashleigh lifted Christina off Shining. "That's probably enough for both of them," Ashleigh said. "It's kind of cold and damp out here."

Christina wailed in protest and struggled in Ashleigh's arms.

"I know, you don't want to stop," Ashleigh said. "I don't blame you, but you'll catch a cold!"

"I'll take her up to the house," Mike offered, coming out of the feed room. "I should help with dinner anyway."

"Thanks." Ashleigh handed Christina to Mike. "Are you guys ready?" she asked Samantha and Cindy, smiling. "It's time to wish the horses a merry Christmas!"

"I'll start with Shining," Cindy said, hurrying to the feed room to get a bucket of sweet feed. When Ashleigh was Cindy's age, she had started the tradition of doing something special for the horses at Christmas, and Cindy had picked up on it. This year each horse would get a couple of handfuls of sweet feed, and Cindy had made everyone a little Christmas tree out of a pine branch, with a gold or silver ornament. Cindy had hung the ornaments carefully near the stalls, out of the horses' reach.

"Merry Christmas, Princess!" Cindy said happily, feeding the mare her treat. Townsend Princess, Wonder's only daughter, had miraculously survived breaking her leg twice. She was in foal to Union Honor, winner of many grade-one stakes races.

Cindy continued on down the row of horses with Ashleigh and Samantha. The mares' lovely heads were all over the stall doors as they waited impatiently for Christmas to come.

"Let's go see the horses in training next," Samantha said after the mares had gotten their treats.

In the large training barn the horses were going stir crazy, Cindy thought. Some were impatiently pawing the ground; others were bumping the half doors with their noses. Shrill whinnies rang out.

"You guys don't understand why we're not going outside today, do you?" Cindy asked. As she passed Wonder's Champion's stall she noticed that the colt was nibbling the wood of his stall door. *I've got to put a stop to that,* she thought. *As soon as I see Storm.*

Storm was waiting patiently in his stall. As usual he was the picture of perfect behavior. Cindy reached into the bucket of sweet feed and handed Storm his treat, then hugged the colt's warm neck. "Since you're the best-behaved horse in the barn, you get to go out with me first," she told him. "Besides, we've got to get you ready to take on those Derby contenders in your next race."

Cindy gave Storm an extra handful of sweet feed because he had been so good, then glanced down the aisle while the colt contentedly munched. *The barn really does look great,* she thought, smiling as her eye traveled down the line of festive little Christmas trees she had made.

Suddenly her smiled vanished. "Oh, no! Where's Champion's Christmas tree?" Cindy rushed to the chestnut colt's stall.

The Christmas tree wasn't in the barn aisle or on the stall floor. In fact, Cindy didn't see any sign of it.

"What's the matter?" Samantha asked in surprise.

"I think Champion ate his Christmas tree—even the ornament!" Cindy said frantically.

"He doesn't look sick." Ashleigh was by Cindy's side.

"No, he doesn't." Wonder's Champion was looking out of his stall with a rather wicked expression, Cindy thought. He had stopped chewing on the door the moment they approached.

Cindy looked in the stall again. "There it is," she said with relief. Champion had gently laid his Christmas tree in his feed box. The ornament was still intact. "How did he do that?" she wondered aloud.

"He's so smart, it's almost uncanny," Ashleigh said. "I wish he would use his intelligence to perform on the track instead of thinking up tricks."

"He will." Cindy fondly patted the colt, still trying to catch her breath after her scare. *He can't help having an ornery side to his disposition,* she thought.

Vic passed the stall with a wheelbarrow. "Merry Christmas!" he called cheerfully.

"Same to you!" Ashleigh replied.

Wonder's Champion leaned over the stall door and laid back his ears. Showing his teeth, he reached out to nip Vic. Vic backed up.

"Champion!" Cindy swatted the colt on the neck. "What gets into you?" It was one thing to think ornery thoughts and another to go around biting people!

"He really doesn't like me," Vic said. "I swear I don't know why."

"Some horses and people don't click," Ashleigh said. "I wouldn't worry about it. But Champion, you'd better settle down."

Champion sulked at the back of his stall, his tail turned to Cindy. *Maybe I was too mean to him*, Cindy thought. But after a few moments the colt turned abruptly around and ventured forward again. Pushing his muzzle into Cindy's hands, he seemed to apologize. "I forgive you," Cindy said, tracing the snip on his nose. "After all, it's Christmas. But what are we going to do with you?"

Champion really knows what he likes and what he doesn't like, and he wants to get his way, Cindy thought as she walked to the stallion barn to wish Glory a merry Christmas. *I'm still sure that much spirit will make him a great racehorse—if I can just figure out how to control it.*

6

"UP, BOY," CINDY SAID TO STORM AS SHE GUIDED HIM onto the ramp of Whitebrook's six-horse trailer. Blanketed against the early January frost, Storm looked like a puff of dark smoke against the light gray horizon. The colt easily climbed the familiar ramp. Mr. Wonderful and four allowance horses were already loaded in the trailer. The horses and Ashleigh, Mike, and Ian were headed to Gulfstream Park, near Miami, for the winter races. Mr. Wonderful would be the first Whitebrook horse to race, in a grade-three stakes in about two weeks.

Cindy latched the trailer gate shut behind Storm. "See you soon, boy," she said. "Be good for Ashleigh, like you always are." Ashleigh would be exercising Storm and Mr. Wonderful on the Gulfstream track, bringing them up to form for race day.

"I think we're ready," Ashleigh said, swinging into the driver's seat of the truck next to Mike.

Christina was staying with Ashleigh's parents at their farm.

"Bye, honey." Ian kissed the top of Cindy's head and climbed into the truck.

With a lump in her throat Cindy watched the gleaming metal van pull out of the drive. She hated to see Storm go. She had never been separated from the colt before, and this was the time when he might need her the most—he was facing his toughest opposition yet. *I'll see him in just a couple of weeks,* she reminded herself. Cindy would fly down with Samantha and Beth on Friday night a week before the race.

She felt a prickle of excitement at the thought of the gray colt running again, showing his trademark blazing speed. *Whatever happens in the race, I know Storm will run his heart out,* she thought.

The following two weeks passed quickly for Cindy with Mike, Ashleigh, and Ian gone. Cindy set her alarm clock to four o'clock instead of five every morning to have enough time to feed and groom the horses and muck out their stalls before school. Samantha helped her, also rising extra early to work in the barns.

Cindy enjoyed her new responsibilities with the horses. As she made her way to the stable before dawn every morning, carefully avoiding the black ice that covered the paths, she heard the calls of the eager horses waiting for her and smiled to herself.

"Don't wear yourself out," Len cautioned one morning as Cindy piled fresh straw in Wonder's Champion's stall.

"I won't." Cindy briskly dusted off her hands and unclipped the colt from the crossties. She had already worked her extra chores into a smooth routine so that she could get them all done and still get to the school bus on time. "I'll put Champion in the paddock," she added.

"Here comes Limitless," Samantha called, bringing Limitless Time out of his stall ahead of Cindy.

On the way out of the barn Cindy stopped Champion by Storm's stall. *It looks so empty*, she thought. Cindy had cleaned the stall out perfectly the day he left, and nothing had disturbed it since. "I wonder how you're doing, Storm," she murmured. "I miss you so much. I love it when you race, but I can't wait for you to come home."

Champion pulled hard on the lead rope and tossed his head. Then he looked eagerly at Cindy.

"Okay, okay—I get the message, Champion," she said with a laugh. "I'll see Storm soon, but I've got to deal with you now. We're going!"

The next Friday night Cindy stared out the small window as the plane taxied into the Miami airport. She couldn't see much in the dark, but the pilot had just said it was seventy degrees in Miami. "I'm so glad to get out of snowy Kentucky," Cindy to Samantha, who was in the seat beside her.

"Yeah, I've had about enough of winter," Samantha agreed. "I was born here in Miami—I don't think I'll ever get used to months of cold."

"I'm just glad we're on the ground," Beth said. She closed the magazine she was reading and looked over at Cindy. "Cindy, honey, it's midnight. I know you want to see the horses, but let's go to the stables tomorrow."

"We could just stop by for a minute," Cindy protested. That would be better than nothing, she thought. She could at least get to see Storm.

Cindy's mother yawned. "You're keeping me up as much as Kevin!" Kevin was staying with Christina at Ashleigh's parents' farm while Beth was at the races.

"We'll wake up the horses if we go see them tonight, Cindy," Samantha said quickly. "We can get up early tomorrow."

"Okay." Cindy was a little disappointed, but that made sense, she admitted to herself.

Outside the airport, Beth hailed a taxi. As they drove along the night streets of Miami to their hotel, Cindy tried to see everything she could. Lush palm trees grew alongside the road. Neon purple, green, and pink lights flashed the briliant, cheerful massage of a lively big city.

At the hotel Beth checked them in at the front desk. "I'm going to go for a walk along the beach," Samantha said. "Want to come, Cindy?"

"Sure—I'm not at all sleepy," Cindy said.

"Make it a short walk, girls, or you'll be exhausted for the race tomorrow," Beth said.

Cindy followed Samantha behind the hotel to the white sand beach. She could hear the soft slap of the waves of the Atlantic Ocean, and a three-quarter, hazy moon lit the water in a glowing path. *I could almost walk on that path,* Cindy thought as she slipped off her shoes. *Does it mean Mr. Wonderful will follow the path to victory tomorrow?* She smiled to herself.

"Mr. Wonderful's last work was fantastic," Samantha said, almost as if she were reading Cindy's mind. "He's going into the race tomorrow the heavy favorite."

"He should win," Cindy said.

Samantha looked out beyond the beach to the moonlit water. "If he stays sound," she said quietly.

Cindy frowned. She knew that was a big if after the colt's injury last year. "I wish Wonder and her offspring didn't get hurt so much," she said. Wonder's racing career had ended when she fractured a cannon bone.

"Mr. Wonderful runs like Wonder, too," Samantha said.

"I know." Cindy bent to let silky sand run through her fingers. "Champion looks like Wonder, but he seems stronger. Maybe he won't get hurt."

"He'd be the perfect horse if he was sound and ran the way Wonder did," Samantha confirmed.

"At least Storm doesn't have health problems," Cindy said. "And he's so fast." She smiled, imagining how happy the colt would be to see her tomorrow. "He's already the perfect horse."

*   *   *

"Work Storm a half!" Mike called down to Ashleigh two days later from the trainers' viewing stand at Gulfstream Park. Cindy stood with Samantha beside Mike, Ian, and several other trainers.

Ashleigh had just passed the viewing stand, riding Storm. The splendid gray colt was trotting so lightly, he seemed suspended in the air. The brilliant sunshine flooding the track glistened on his sleek coat. "Okay!" Ashleigh waved to Mike.

Cindy leaned over the rail. "Go get 'em, Storm!" she called. She wanted to add, *Like Mr. Wonderful did yesterday in the Broward!* but she didn't want to brag in front of the other trainers.

Mr. Wonderful had won his race decisively yesterday, leading wire to wire and drawing off in the stretch to a six-length victory. Cindy's throat still hurt from cheering the colt on. He had come out of the race beautifully, with no sign of injury.

Now it's Storm's turn, Cindy thought excitedly. In just six days Storm would be out there on the Gulfstream track, racing in the Holy Bull Stakes.

"All right, Storm!" Cindy yelled.

Storm slowed at Cindy's words and turned his head, searching the track for her. Cindy knew that horses seldom looked up, and Storm couldn't find her. But Cindy was sure he knew she was there. She was positive there was an extra bounce to the colt's strides as he and Ashleigh continued on their way at a brisk trot.

About twenty horses in the second set were walking, trotting, or galloping on the track. The first set had already gone back to the barn. The trainers occasionally called out instructions but mostly stood quietly, intently following their horses' performance on the track.

"Storm really missed you riding him, Cindy," Samantha said. "I thought he wasn't going to let you leave him this morning."

"I know! I felt the same way." Cindy realized that it had been hard on Storm to be separated from his familiar rider and groom. The colt had been disobedient for almost the first time in his life that morning when Ashleigh had asked him to walk onto the track, without Cindy. He had stopped dead when he realized Cindy wasn't coming and whinnied. Ashleigh had to urge him forward.

Cindy lifted her binoculars to follow Storm on the far side of the track. Ashleigh had picked up Storm's trot to a slow gallop. Crouching farther over Storm's neck, she asked him for more. Storm responded instantly, his long legs reaching for ground and easily putting it away. As the colt swept past the viewing stand in full gear, his mane and tail whipping straight out behind him, he looked like a flying gray streamer.

Cindy wanted to laugh out loud with happiness. *He's just so beautiful!* she thought.

"Look at Storm go." Samantha shook her head in amazement. "I'd like to see the time for that half."

Ashleigh slowed the colt at the gap, turning him

back toward the viewing stand and ending his workout.

"We'll be seeing that one in black type," Mike said. Cindy knew that the fastest workout of the day would appear in bold type in the racing publications.

Cindy hurried down the steps of the viewing stand to meet Ashleigh and Storm. "Way to go, boy!" she called to the colt.

Storm was breathing lightly and his neck was hardly marred with sweat, despite the warm temperatures. When he saw Cindy, he whinnied loudly.

"I'm here!" she reassured him, taking his reins. "We'll go to the barn together."

Ashleigh dismounted and pushed back her dark hair. "Wow, it was hot out there! I'm still not used to it. I think I'm sweating more than Storm."

"What did you think of Storm's work?" Cindy asked eagerly.

"It was fine," Ashleigh said. But Cindy caught the hesitation in Ashleigh's voice.

"What's the matter?" she asked anxiously. Storm was resting his head on her shoulder, as if he didn't have a care in the world now that they were together.

"Nothing." Ashleigh shook her head. "I just don't think we're going to walk away with Storm's race, the way we did with Mr. Wonderful in the Broward."

"Why not?" Cindy stroked Storm's neck, enjoying its fine gray silkiness. She'd had her doubts about Storm running in another long race. But the colt's excellent condition and this morning's stunning workout had made her optimistic about his chances. "Do you the other horses will run faster than he just did on race day?"

"No, I don't." Ashleigh hesitated again. "At least not for a half mile. But we'll find out on Saturday."

The day before Storm's race, Samantha took Cindy and Ashleigh on a tour of Miami. "It'll keep us from thinking too much about tomorrow," she said.

They stopped at a novelty store to look for gifts. Cindy touched a tray of seashells displayed on a counter. *Maybe Kevin and Christina would like some of those to play with,* she thought. Cindy turned to ask Ashleigh and Samantha their opinion and saw that they were deep in conversation.

As Cindy approached they stopped talking. But Cindy was sure she had heard the word *Storm.* "What? Please tell me what you were talking about," Cindy begged. "It was about Storm, wasn't it?"

"Yes, we were discussing the race tomorrow." Ashleigh looked troubled.

"Tell her," Samantha said. "She should know."

"Okay." Ashleigh took a deep breath. "I don't want to worry you, Cindy, but the Holy Bull is going to be a tough race. The Kentucky Jockey Club was probably even harder on Storm than it looked. I had to ask him for everything he had—and then some. We still just barely pulled it off. And the competition for the Holy Bull has just gotten stiffer and stiffer. I think every Kentucky Derby hopeful on the East Coast is entered. Two more entered last week. It's going to be a huge field."

"That doesn't sound good. Maybe you should scratch Storm," Samantha said.

"No, I don't really want to do that." Ashleigh frowned. "Maybe if I have a good ride, and Storm throws his heart into the race the way he always does, we can win. But this race will definitely be pivotal in deciding at what distance he should race in the future."

Well, that's not completely bad, Cindy consoled herself, wandering back to the shells. *If Storm loses the Holy Bull, he can just go back to sprints, and we know he can win those.* She absently picked up a superb conch, rosy pink inside and with as many turrets as a castle. *I'll get this shell for Christina,* she decided. *But I wonder why Ashleigh's so worried about Storm?*

After a delicious seafood dinner at a restaurant overlooking one of Miami's canals, Samantha drove them back to the track. "I'm going to see Storm," Cindy said as she got out of the car. Ashleigh's words about the race had made her a little uneasy. She wanted to see the colt again and check his condition for herself.

"We'll come, too," Ashleigh said. "I want to look at Mr. Wonderful and the other horses."

In the barn Storm had his lovely dark gray head over the stall door. He seemed to be waiting for

Cindy. "I missed you, too," Cindy said, pressing her cheek to his. "But you don't have to worry when I go. I'm back for a while now."

Storm whickered, as if he were asking a question. "No, I'm not leaving you tonight, either," Cindy told him. "I'll spend the night here. I'm just going to get a cot out of the feed room."

Storm bobbed his head, his eyes bright. He seemed in complete agreement with her plan.

Cindy buried her face in his mane. "I won't ever leave you when you need me." Storm looked wonderful to her, but what Ashleigh had said still bothered her. *I sure hope Storm's ready for tomorrow,* she thought.

"So you're staying tonight?" Len asked, coming up in the feed room as Cindy dug behind the hay bales for the cot.

"Yes—if Mom and Dad will let me. But they usually do." Cindy had spent the night in Glory's stall last year when she had been afraid he would be drugged before one of his races. She had also stayed with Glory before the Breeders' Cup Classic. Cindy knew that her parents worried she didn't get enough sleep in the stall, and so she tried to stay there only when it was critical. This seemed like one of those times.

Len nodded understandingly. "You being here might be just what Storm needs. A lot of what goes into that colt's running style is mental."

Storm watched closely as Cindy unfolded the cot

in the stall. "There," she said. "Now I'll just go get a blanket and talk to Mom and Dad. Then we'll be all set."

Storm nosed the cot curiously. It toppled on its side and he backed away, snorting. "Just don't do that when I'm asleep on it," Cindy warned, smiling as she set up the cot again. She sat down on it to see what Storm would do.

The gray colt stepped cautiously forward and sniffed the cot. Then he sniffed Cindy's hands and sighed deeply. He seemed to be saying, Whatever you want is fine with me.

"This will be fun for both of us," Cindy said, reaching up to run her hands through the colt's gray mane. "And I hope it helps you tomorrow." *Because you may need all the help you can get,* she thought.

7

Cindy turned over restlessly. But the soft, insistent tickling on her cheek didn't stop. "Go away," she mumbled, trying to move away on the narrow cot.

The tickling changed to a firm nudge, and the cot almost flipped over. Cindy abruptly sat up straight and rubbed her eyes. She looked up as Storm spooked and jumped to the back of the stall.

"Hey, you," Cindy said playfully. Sunlight spilled in the door, and the air was already warm. "How come nobody woke me up but you?" she asked the colt. "It must be eight o'clock."

Ian looked over the stall door. "Morning, sleepyhead. Did Storm keep you awake?"

"No, not at all." Cindy was amazed that all the early morning stable noise hadn't woken her. "Why didn't you get me up?"

"You two looked so comfortable in there." Ian smiled. "Storm slept late, too."

73

"I'll walk him around the yard now and start getting him ready for the race," Cindy said, throwing back her covers. She was wide awake now.

After she had quickly washed up and dressed, Cindy put Storm in crossties and collected his brushes. "You look gorgeous," she told the colt proudly.

Cindy carefully worked over Storm's smooth gray coat for half an hour, then stepped back to admire him. Storm glistened dark silver in the morning sun, and his muscles rippled with conditioning. He seemed ready to take on the world.

I hope he comes out of the race all right, Cindy thought. She wondered if Storm would be exhausted again, the way he had been after the Kentucky Jockey Club. She hoped her extra work with him this winter would pay off.

Storm yawned and rubbed the side of his head against her hands. "You're pretty relaxed for race day," Cindy said, rubbing his ears. "And you must know you're going to race, because you didn't get as much to eat as usual this morning."

I'd like to ask Dad or Ashleigh what they think about him, Cindy decided, unclipping the colt from the crossties. But no one was around the barn except for Len, whistling as he cleaned stalls. Cindy knew Len was just as partial to Storm as she was. He always thought the colt looked fine.

"Let's go for a walk," she said to Storm. "We can limber you up and see if we can find Dad or Ashleigh."

74

Cindy first checked the viewing stand, which was just behind the barns. Several other trainers were up there, watching their horses on the track, but no one from Whitebrook.

Cindy turned Storm to walk in front of the neatly painted green and white shedrows. Ian or Ashleigh might be there, talking to another trainer. She stopped in front of barn 9.

"That's the Misty Ridge stabling," Cindy murmured. Misty Ridge, a New York–based stable, would be running Storm's main competition in the Holy Bull Stakes: Alyba and Torte Finale. The stable was the focus of attention in the Thoroughbred industry this year since both horses were considered hot Derby prospects.

Cindy felt a little envious. Mr. Wonderful was getting a lot of attention again after his victory in the Broward last week. But he wouldn't be running in the Triple Crown races, since he was four and those races were only for three-year-olds. *It would be so exciting to have a Triple Crown prospect*, she thought.

An older man walked out of one of the Misty Ridge stalls, leading a superbly muscled bay. *That's Alyba!* Cindy realized. The colt looked like formidable competition, and Cindy found it hard to take her eyes off him. *But I'd better not hang around*, she thought, turning Storm to take him to the next shedrow. She wasn't sure she would be welcome here.

"Hello there," the man called as he led Alyba over to where Cindy was standing.

"Hi," Cindy said hesitantly. She recognized him now as Nick Sayer, Misty Ridge's head trainer.

"You're Ian McLean's daughter, aren't you?" Nick asked pleasantly.

Cindy nodded. "I was just looking at Alyba—he's incredible. But I don't want to bother you."

Nick laughed. "Go ahead and look. That won't change the outcome of the race."

Storm stretched his neck toward the other horse and whickered. Alyba returned the greeting, but Cindy kept Storm and Alyba well apart. She knew that colts often had unpredictable moods.

Nick lightly sprayed Alyba's back with a hose. The colt grunted and pulled away. "Now, enough of that," Nick said. "Here comes your friend."

A groom led a short black and white goat up to the colt. The two animals touched noses, and Alyba relaxed, standing quietly.

"Well, I have to get going," Cindy said. "Thank you."

"No problem," Nick said and waved. "Say hi to your dad."

On the way back to the Whitebrook shedrow Cindy saw Ian and Mike in the trainer's viewing stand. Ashleigh would be riding Mr. Wonderful on the track for his morning workout, Cindy realized.

"Let's just go to our shedrow," she said to Storm. "They'll be back soon. I'll stay with you until the race."

Storm flicked his ears and leaned closer to her. He

seemed to be saying that was what he would like the most.

Some horses have a goat companion and some have a person, Cindy thought, smiling. *I can't imagine a better friend than Storm, either.*

That afternoon the saddling paddock bustled with activity as trainers, grooms, and owners readied their horses for the Holy Bull Stakes. "I never saw so many people in the paddock before," Cindy said to Len.

"A lot of these horses have multiple owners," Len said as he picked up Storm's racing saddle.

"And I guess they all showed up," Cindy said. She watched Len smooth Storm's special saddlecloth over the saddle pad and step back. She felt a quick thrill of pride as she read Storm's name.

Len lifted the saddle over Storm's back. The colt shied away from him and snorted. "Easy, big guy," Len soothed.

Cindy looked at Storm in surprise. He had never acted up in the saddling paddock before. "I think all this confusion is bothering him," she said, touching Storm's flank with a reassuring hand.

"I'll hang on tight to him," Len said as he led Storm into the walking ring.

Storm snorted, showing the whites of his eyes. Len quickly led him around the ring, staying clear of the other horses. Torte Finale, the other Misty Ridge Stable entry, was pacing calmly beside his groom and Nick Sayer.

Cindy glanced at Storm. His neck was arched, and he was pulling at the lead much more than he usually did. He looked beautiful, but upset.

A huge crowd surrounded the walking ring. The Florida sun was brilliant and hot in the clear blue sky, but a cooling breeze lifted Storm's long mane and tail.

"It's a great day to be at the races," Len said calmly.

Cindy nodded. She saw Ian, Ashleigh, and Mike approaching from the far end of the ring. *I'd better tell Ashleigh how wired Storm is,* Cindy thought. Then she realized that the experienced jockey would see that herself.

"Why are you acting like this, Storm?" Cindy muttered as the colt plunged toward the rail of the walking ring. Len quickly pulled him away. Shaking his head, the colt pranced lithely between them. "Save it for the race!" Cindy said.

Cindy sat down next to Samantha in the section of the stands reserved for Whitebrook. Storm had just stepped onto the track for the post parade.

Despite her worries Cindy felt her spirits rise as the glorious colt marched by the onlookers, his exquisite head held high. "He's a beauty," Samantha commented.

"He sure is," Cindy said. Storm stopped and looked around, his nostrils flaring. Ashleigh leaned forward to pat the colt and seemed to be talking to him. "I'm glad Storm drew the one position," Cindy added.

"Yeah, that should help," Samantha agreed.

"The track's been favoring closers for the past couple of days," Ian remarked.

"Ashleigh knows," Mike replied. "She's going to try to rate Storm again, the way she did in the Jockey Club."

"Storm closed then," Cindy said, and felt a surge of hope.

"He sure did." Beth looked around Mike and Samantha and smiled at Cindy.

"Alyba has a strong closing kick," Mike said. "So does Torte Finale. This is going to be an interesting race."

I think Storm can win, Cindy told herself. *He did so well in the Kentucky Jockey Club.*

The seven horses in the field loaded quickly in the gate. The afternoon sun shone on the still horses, making them look as if they were frozen in amber.

The next second the bell rang shrilly, and Storm exploded from the gate. He already had a full stride on the rest of the field!

"And it's Storm's Ransom, showing early speed in this race," the announcer called.

Cindy jumped up, twisting her hands with excitement. She couldn't believe how fast Storm was running already. In seconds he had drawn away to a four-length lead! "Go, boy!" Cindy cheered.

She glanced at the other faces around her and saw only worry. "What's the matter?" she asked.

Samantha pointed at the board. "Look at the fraction he set for the first quarter mile."

Cindy tore her gaze from the track. "Wow!" she said in amazement. "Isn't that almost a record time?"

"Yes, but Storm can't keep it up!" Ian shook his head. "Look at the board—he just set a faster fraction for the last quarter mile!"

"Glory did that in the Classic," Cindy reminded him. She strained to see Storm's action, then picked up her binoculars. The gray colt was running smoothly along the backstretch, his legs churning pistons of power. Cindy saw that he was maintaining his lead of four lengths.

The punishing pace had put most of the field away already, but Alyba and Torte Finale were almost neck and neck behind Storm and showed no signs of slowing. Cindy knew that as closers, the two Misty Ridge colts were still very much in contention in the race.

"Storm's not Glory." Mike's voice was tense.

No, but he's a great horse, too! Cindy thought. Even from a distance she could see how much Storm was extended as he rounded the far turn. But the wire was still a quarter mile away, and Cindy could tell that Storm was tiring. His strides weren't nearly as fluid as they had been in the first part of the race, and his tail was flicking in distress. He was keeping up his blazing speed, but with a sinking sensation, Cindy realized he was just trying to go too fast. In a split second Storm dropped his pace, and Alyba and Torte Finale roared up to close.

"There go Alyba and Torte Finale," Samantha said. "Storm's going to have to find another gear!"

"Please kick in, Storm!" Cindy cried. "You can do it!" She could almost feel Storm's effort as the colt changed leads and valiantly reached for ground. But in her heart she knew he would come up short. Alyba and Torte Finale swept by Storm in the stretch, battling each other for first.

"A photo for first and second," the announcer called. "And Storm's Ransom is a well-beaten third."

Tears blurred Cindy's eyes and she wiped them away. How could Storm try so hard and finish third?

I wonder if he's all right! she thought. Not waiting for the rest of the group to file out of their seats, Cindy climbed over the railing behind them and ran down to the track.

Alyba was stepping behind Nick Sayer into the winner's circle, but Cindy hardly noticed. She searched the track for Storm. Ashleigh was trotting him slowly back along the stretch. She pulled up the colt and dismounted.

"Oh, Storm!" Cindy realized in horror just how badly the race had gone. The colt was trembling all over from exhaustion and stress. *He looks even worse than he did after the Kentucky Jockey Club!* Cindy thought. She quickly ran to Storm's side. The colt whickered once, barely audibly, and hung his head.

"Let's get him back to the barn," Ashleigh said. Cindy had never seen her look more worried. "He's had it for today."

"What happened?" Cindy asked as Mike, Ian, and the rest of the Whitebrook group joined them. Mike and Ian began looking the colt over carefully.

"I'm not sure what the problem was." Ashleigh frowned. "Storm set those burning early fractions and used himself up. I tried to rate him, but he just wouldn't have it."

"I don't think he can handle a mile and a sixteenth," Mike said.

Cindy began to lead Storm to the backside, keeping protectively close to her horse. "What did I do wrong?" she asked miserably. Cindy thought how carefully she had tried to condition Storm that winter.

"Nothing, Cindy," Ashleigh said. "Our instincts were probably right—Storm just isn't a distance horse."

"I almost think—" Cindy gulped. "He was so wired before the race. He seemed to know how hard he was going to have to try."

"Maybe he did." Ashleigh looked sadly at the downcast colt. "If he were human, I'd say he was heartbroken. I'm sorry, Cindy. I should have known this race wasn't a good idea. We'll try him in a sprint next time."

If there is a next time, Cindy thought. Fear gripped her heart as she looked at Storm. His eyes were dull and tired, and when she touched his neck, it was sopping wet. *Storm's so sensitive. His racing career really may be over!*

"But I'm not going to give up on you," she said softly. "We'll get through this, Storm—I promise."

8

AT THE END OF JANUARY THE WEATHER IN KENTUCKY warmed, and the snow melted. Cindy walked to the training barn, sniffing the clean scent from the wet ground and smiling for almost the first time since Storm's loss a week ago in the Holy Bull. Right after school Ashleigh had stopped by the McLeans' cottage and asked Cindy to tack up Wonder's Champion. The colt was going back into training.

I can hardly wait, she thought. Champion had grown and filled out in the two months since she had ridden him. Cindy wondered how fast he would be. *Maybe*, she thought, *he'll be Wonder's fastest offspring yet.*

Champion was looking impatiently out of his stall, his eyes almost black in his chocolate-colored face. "You look ready to get out," Cindy said, taking a lead from the nail on the wall and opening the stall door.

Len came up behind her. "I longed him for a while under tack," he said. "Just to get the kinks out of him."

"Thanks." Cindy knew that if Champion wasn't longed before she rode him, she might have to sit out a lot of bucks and hops while the lively colt worked off his excess energy.

Champion marched out of his stall without waiting for her to tell him where they were going. Cindy caught up and quickly clipped him in the crossties. "Do you think you could wait for me?" she asked him.

The colt bobbed his head. He seemed to be saying that he knew perfectly well where he was going—the track, and that it more than suited him.

"Just let me brush you a minute," Cindy said. Len would have already brushed the colt, but Cindy could see bits of straw in his mane and tail. Obviously he had just taken a good roll in his stall.

Cindy sighed as she thoroughly brushed out Champion's dark brown tail. She was glad the colt was in such good spirits. Storm, she knew, still wasn't.

Ashleigh had been at the Gulfstream track with Storm until yesterday. She had said that he seemed to be recovering physically, but his heart wasn't in his works, and his timings were slow. Mike had entered the colt in the Hutcheson Stakes, a seven-furlong sprint next Sunday, but right now no one was too optimistic about his chances.

Well, I'll be with Storm tomorrow, Cindy consoled

herself. She had gotten permission to miss almost a full week of school so that she could spend extra time with the colt at Gulfstream. *I hope I can make a difference,* she thought. Storm responded so well to personal contact, Cindy was sure he would be much happier when she was around.

Wonder's Champion twisted his head and pulled the brush out of her hand with his teeth, snapping her back to reality.

"Are you ready?" Cindy almost laughed at the eager expression in the colt's eyes. "But don't get too excited. We're not going to do much today since it's the first time you've been ridden in a while."

Cindy quickly tacked up Champion and led him out of the barn. The colt pranced after her, obediently staying a pace behind her.

Ashleigh walked up from the mares' paddock. "I was checking on Princess and Shining," she said. "Any day now they'll have their foals."

"I can't wait!" Cindy looked behind Ashleigh and saw the two foals that had been born last week. Their mothers were Right to Run, winner of the Kentucky Oaks, and Talking Lady, full sister to a Derby winner. The little bay and chestnut stood very close to their mothers, but their active ears and eyes were taking in the big new world around them.

Wonder's Champion hauled on the reins, as if to remind Cindy that he wouldn't be second fiddle to anybody, not for an instant.

"Gosh, he's a big guy," Ashleigh said. "He's so

much taller than Wonder already." Ashleigh looked directly at Cindy. "Are you sure your dad will let you ride Champion? I thought he wasn't too keen on the idea."

"Sure, it's okay," Cindy said evasively. She told herself that her dad hadn't forbidden her to ride Champion, at least not directly. He had just taken the colt out of training the last time Champion had run away with her.

Ian was home now from Gulfstream, but Cindy hadn't seen him that afternoon. She hoped wherever he was, he stayed there about an hour longer. Cindy promised herself that she would just try Champion today, then talk to her dad tomorrow about riding him when they all returned to Gulfstream.

"Warm Champion up slowly today," Ashleigh said. "See how he goes at a walk and a trot. I don't think we should try a gallop just yet."

Cindy nodded. She was anxious for nothing to go wrong. Wonder's Champion was two now, and everyone would be expecting him to perform better than he had last fall.

She swung lightly into the saddle with a hand from Ashleigh. The colt stood docilely. *Probably Len got on him already today,* Cindy thought, *just to make sure I wouldn't get killed when I tried it.*

Cindy settled into the saddle, smiling at the colt's familiar tug on the reins. A breeze blew Cindy's hair, and she brushed it aside. She could hardly wait to get going.

"Cindy, what are you doing?" Ian called.

Champion shied sideways. Cindy saw her dad approaching the track from the stallion barn.

"As if I didn't know," Ian continued. "I don't want you riding that colt."

"Dad, I have to," Cindy said quickly. "He'll just be worse for anyone else. Besides, he may go perfectly now."

Champion bounced on his feet, clearly bored with standing still. Cindy gave him a warning pull on the reins and circled him to release his tension. Champion wasn't helping her make her case.

"All right, Cindy," Ian said at last, but he didn't look happy. "At the first sign of trouble, though, someone else is going to ride him."

The spirited colt spun in a tight circle, then began backing up. Cindy nudged him with her legs to make him stop. *I have to get him to mind me today so that he can go into serious training*, she thought. If Champion didn't start racing soon, he couldn't win enough races by his three-year-old season to compete in the Triple Crown. Cindy knew she was probably thinking way too far ahead, but she still thought the colt's chances of really being something on the track were good—if he would just put his mind to business.

Cindy guided Champion through the gap and asked him for a brisk walk counterclockwise around the track. The colt set off instantly, but Cindy kept every muscle and nerve alert. The last time Champion had been ridden, he had seen how easy it was to get his way. Cindy wasn't expecting a smooth ride now.

"Mind me today, boy," she said firmly. "You just don't know how important it is."

The colt threw up his head a little, but he settled down. Cindy gave him a little rein, asking for a trot. *He might start acting up if he has to go slowly for too long*, she thought.

The colt's smooth gait was glorious. Cindy felt a smile steal across her face. She could sense the colt's coiled energy as he floated across the track, as if no surface were beneath him. His strides were big and even as he trotted along.

Cindy was still watching him carefully. She saw that the big colt was watching her, too, rolling his dark eyes back until the whites showed. Cindy wondered if he was plotting something.

Don't be ridiculous, she told herself. *Horses don't plot!*

They rounded the far turn and passed the gap. Cindy saw that Samantha had joined the group, holding Kevin. "Just keep doing what you're doing," Ashleigh called to Cindy. "Take him around two more times, then we'll quit for today. He looks good!"

Cindy felt her cheeks warm at Ashleigh's praise. She reached down to pat Champion's neck.

At that instant Kevin let out a loud cry. Champion stopped dead, bracing all four feet, and stared at the baby.

Cindy shifted in the saddle, quickly regaining her balance from the sudden stop. Before she could take up on the reins, the colt wheeled and broke into a dead run, heading back around the track.

No, please don't let this be happening again! Cindy desperately pulled on the reins. But Champion was accelerating in great bursts of speed, shooting past the white inside rail. A marker post flashed by them. *We've already gone a quarter mile!* Cindy thought wildly. Her heart was racing with fear for the colt and for herself. If she made the wrong decision at any second, the consequences could be fatal.

Pulling the reins with all her strength, Cindy managed to keep the colt going in a fairly straight line. The gap loomed before them. *We already lapped the track at a gallop!* Cindy prayed the colt would slow at the usual stopping place. If he just would slow down a little, she might be able to bring him hard around and get him back under control.

Instead, as if he knew her thoughts, Wonder's Champion veered toward the rail.

"He's going to hit the rail—get off him!" Samantha screamed.

Cindy made a split-second decision. The colt was going into the rail, with or without her. But if she stayed with him, she still might be able to slow him at least a little.

The colt smashed into the rail. Cindy felt as if the world were moving in slow motion as Champion fell to his knees, then rolled onto his side. Cindy flew off sideways onto the turf course. She just had time to thank her lucky stars that the colt wasn't falling on her before she hit the ground.

Ohhhhhh! Cindy screamed silently. She had taken the full force of impact on her left arm, the one she had broken two years ago in a collision with Wonder's Pride. The pain was almost making her black out. *I've broken my arm again!* she thought frantically. *I won't be able to ride for weeks!*

But worse than that fear was her terror for Champion. He had fallen so hard! "Champion!" she cried. The colt was already on his feet. He was standing on all four legs, so at least they weren't broken. But Cindy stared in horror at blood trickling from the colt's shoulder.

Ian, Ashleigh, Samantha, and Vic were already running across the track toward her. "Are you all right?" Ian asked anxiously.

"Yeah, I guess." Cindy's head was swimming. She pushed herself up off the soft dirt and managed to stand unsteadily.

"Call the vet, Sammy!" Ian cried. "And please get me some clean cloths from the barn." Samantha handed off Kevin to Vic and set off at a dead run for the barn.

"Oh, Champion," Cindy cried. "I'm so sorry. This is my fault."

"Don't say that," Ashleigh said calmly. "You couldn't have done any better than you did. Help me hold him still, Cindy."

Cindy reached up for the colt's bridle with her left hand and almost cried out from the pain.

"Try to move your fingers," Ashleigh said, her voice quiet but urgent. Ian ran in quickly to hold the colt.

Slowly Cindy wiggled her fingers. She could do it, but the pain was so bad, she sank down onto the ground again. She forced back her tears. The situation was bad enough without her crying. It was her responsibility to keep the colt safe, and she hadn't done it.

Champion stepped closer to her, pulling Ian and Ashleigh with him. Cindy looked up and saw that she wasn't the only one who was being brave about the fall. Champion was stretching his nose toward her, as if he wanted to know if she was all right.

Or maybe he was just looking for his usual caress after a ride. Cindy could hardly believe it. All the horses she had ever known would have been thoroughly shaken after a fall like that. Champion was acting like nothing had happened.

He got his way again, she thought with frustration.

"I'm not going to stitch this," Dr. Smith said as she examined Champion's shoulder. She had arrived at Whitebrook within ten minutes of Samantha's call. Ian and Ashleigh were still holding the colt out on the track. They hadn't wanted to move him and risk further injury. "It's a superficial wound—it looks worse than it is," Dr. Smith added. "I'll just bandage

91

it and give Champion a tetanus shot to prevent infection. You can put on some ointment, too. It should heal right up."

"That colt needs a new nickname," Ian said. Cindy saw that her dad still looked upset. "'Champion' doesn't describe him. 'Troublemaker' would be better."

Max made a sympathetic face at Cindy. He had come on the call with his mother when he heard that Wonder's Champion was injured.

"But it's his name," Cindy ventured. She had barely managed to talk Ian out of rushing her to the doctor before Champion was taken care of. Her dad wanted to see if she had a hairline fracture or other injuries. Cindy could feel her wrist starting to swell.

"Cindy, you're not riding him anymore," Ian said firmly. "This time I mean it. Vic or Mark will ride him."

Cindy tightened her lips. *I have to ride Champion!* she thought. *He trusts me. He'll just go worse for Vic and Mark. He'll get hurt again or hurt somebody, and then Dad will sell him!*

"Cindy, you've got to be careful," Ashleigh said gently. "You just took a bad fall. If you'd broken that arm again, you might not have been able to ride anymore."

Cindy was silent. She didn't want to admit it, but she understood what Ashleigh was saying. Cindy didn't want her riding career to be over.

Champion was watching her hopefully. Cindy

managed a wry smile. "I wonder what his time was out there?" she said.

"Fast." Ashleigh gave Cindy a look of understanding. "We've got to find a way to channel that speed."

"I know." Cindy rubbed her forehead with her right hand. She had to find a way to get through to the headstrong colt—soon.

"I guess I shouldn't have brought Kevin up to the track," Samantha said. "But Champion's seen him before. I don't understand why he took off like that."

"I think Champion spooked on purpose," Cindy said tentatively. She looked up to see where her dad was. Dr. Smith was administering the tetanus shot while her dad and Max held the colt. "He did it for fun, and because he felt like running," she continued quietly. "I don't think he meant to go into the rail—he just didn't want to do what I told him. But I don't think he'll ever go into the rail like that again." She looked at Ashleigh. "Does it sound crazy to think a horse could be that smart?"

"Not for Wonder's son." Ashleigh shook her head. "She's smart, too."

"But Champion's not like Wonder." Cindy sighed, thinking of Wonder's sweet disposition.

"No, he's more like his sire or grandsire," Ashleigh agreed. "I think he got that pigheadedness from them. Townsend Victor, his sire, was always a handful. He had to be retired after an injury that I think would have been preventable if he hadn't been out of control at the time. Champion's grandsire, Star Way, also had a real reputation as a troublemaker on the track."

"So he inherited their stubbornness," Cindy said. Glory had inherited all kinds of fantastic qualities from his grandfather, Just Victory. She wished Champion had inherited something good from his father or grandfather.

"Yes, but Champion inherited their speed, too." Ashleigh looked thoughtful. "Let's try this, Cindy," she said after a moment. "Ian doesn't want you to ride, but you could walk Champion around the track and stable yard. He seems to get overexcited about little things, and because he's so strong, the consequences are disastrous. I also think the more he bonds with you, the better you'll be able to control him on the track."

"Okay," Cindy said, relieved Ashleigh wasn't giving up on the colt or assigning him to another rider. "Storm loves it when I walk with him," she added. "Maybe that really would work with this guy, too."

Cindy didn't want to try riding Champion again until she was sure that he wouldn't throw her. But at the same time she didn't want to quit on the colt. Every time she rode him, he treated her to a few blissful moments of speed, grace, and power unlike any she'd ever experienced on a horse, except maybe Glory. Cindy still hoped that someday Champion would be a great racehorse. She could tell that Ashleigh felt the same way.

Cindy walked over to her dad, who was trying to hold Champion. The high-strung colt was squirming and shaking his head. "I'll take him back to the barn," Cindy offered.

"Are you sure?" Ian asked. Cindy nodded.

Champion dropped his head to sniff Cindy's hand, and Cindy rubbed his blaze. "I guess you're worth all this trouble. But you're a long way from the Triple Crown, boy," she said ruefully.

Champion snorted indignantly, as if to say, *I* don't have any doubts.

9

"THERE HE IS!" CINDY SAID DELIGHTEDLY. STORM HAD JUST walked to the gap of the Gulfstream track with Ashleigh up. He was finishing a workout in preparation for the Hutcheson Stakes in six days. An hour ago Cindy and Ian had flown into the Miami airport and driven straight to the track, but Cindy hadn't had a chance to greet Storm. Ashleigh and Mike had arrived on an earlier flight that day. Beth, Kevin, and Christina would join the group the day before the race.

Storm was walking quietly for Ashleigh—*too quietly for a horse that just worked*, Cindy thought, her spirits sinking. Storm still wasn't up to form.

The colt raised his head at the sound of her voice and whinnied joyously. "Oh, I'm glad to see you, too!" Cindy cried, running to him.

Storm bobbed on his front hooves and tucked his head under Cindy's arm. Cindy made sure it was her right one, because her left arm was still painful. By icing it and putting on a good face, Cindy had managed to convince her dad that it was no big deal.

Storm let out a long, quivering sigh. Cindy forgot that anything could be wrong when she was this happy to see her horse. "I'm here, Storm," she reassured him. "I wouldn't miss your next race for anything."

"Hi, Cindy." Ashleigh said. She dismounted and stretched her arms out to Christina, who Mike had brought onto the track. Cindy smiled as Ashleigh, Mike, and Christina shared a big group hug.

"I'll take Storm back to the barn and cool him out," Cindy offered.

"Good idea," Ashleigh said. "I want to rub down his legs really well."

"What was his time out there?" Cindy asked.

Ashleigh's face told Cindy the answer. "Poor," she finally said. "I'm sorry, Cindy, but there's no other way to put it. Maybe he'll perk up now that you're here. Or maybe physically he's just not ready to race. I'm going to give Storm a couple more days, then work him again. But if he goes like he did today, I'll have to scratch him from the race."

What will happen to Storm if he can't race on Sunday? Cindy thought fearfully. Mike, Ian, and Ashleigh would almost certainly lose confidence in his abilities. They might not be quick to give Storm another chance to race. Even selling the colt wasn't out of the question. Storm's bloodlines weren't exceptional, and Cindy doubted if Mike would want to add Storm to the six stallions Whitebrook already had.

Cindy shook her head. She just couldn't let Storm be sold or retired. "Okay, Storm," she said firmly. "We've got work to do."

Over the next few days Cindy spent every minute she could with Storm. She had worked hard to get him ready for the Holy Bull, but for the next race, the Hutcheson, she knew she'd have to do even better.

Every morning she got up before dawn. First she brushed Storm for an hour, even though his smooth, short gray coat barely needed it. The colt loved the deep strokes of the soothing brush and half closed his eyes, leaning into the massage. Next Cindy walked Storm for an hour around the shedrow, letting him relax and enjoy the sweet-scented, warm air of the permanent Florida summer.

Sometimes Ashleigh walked with them, bouncing Christina in a backpack. At first Storm had nuzzled the baby curiously while Christina laughed and patted his nose. Storm seemed to like the baby's attention.

Cindy made a mental note to bring a baby, either Christina or Kevin, to walk with Wonder's Champion when she got home. The next time she rode Champion—and she was determined there would be a next time—she wanted to eliminate babies from his list of things to spook from.

Every other day Ashleigh galloped Storm on the track. Even after the first gallop, Cindy was sure she saw a definite improvement in his attitude. Storm came off the track prancing and snorting. *He looks like a real racehorse,* Cindy thought with satisfaction.

She had slept in the stall for only one night to prepare Storm for the Holy Bull, but now she stayed with him every night. Cindy played her portable CD player and talked to Storm the way she had with Glory during his racing days. She hoped to work the same magic on the dark gray colt.

Storm blossomed under the attention. His coat glowed with an extra sheen, and his gaze was alert and affectionate as he watched Cindy go about her work.

Three days before the Hutcheson, Ashleigh took Storm out for his final work. Leaning on the rail, Cindy watched anxiously as Ashleigh put Storm into a slow gallop.

Cindy frowned. Storm was galloping at a good clip, but he wasn't driving—he hardly seemed to know he was on a racetrack. The difference was painfully clear when she looked at Mr. Wonderful, galloping under Samantha on the other side of the track. The moment a breezing colt passed Mr. Wonderful, Samantha had her hands full to hold the colt. But Storm good-naturedly let all the other horses pass, making no effort to catch them.

Ashleigh stopped Storm in front of Cindy and shook her head. "Cindy, I think I'm going to have to scratch him."

Cindy swallowed hard. "I guess he isn't going very well." She couldn't try to talk Ashleigh out of scratching Storm if Ashleigh thought the colt wouldn't fire. If Storm lost again, Cindy was sure they could never bring him back.

"He's still not quite up to form," Ashleigh said as she leaned forward and rubbed Storm's neck. "I thought he might have a mental thing about trying to win after his loss in the Holy Bull, so I galloped him with our two allowance horses. I thought if he won against them, it might restore his confidence. Storm pulled even, but he didn't try to win."

Desperately Cindy racked her mind. She had done so much for Storm, and he had improved a lot. But she knew that very few horses were stakes caliber. She had to come up with something to give Storm that extra edge.

Her eyes widened. "Run Storm against Mr. Wonderful at a half mile," she said, trying to sound sure of herself.

Ashleigh looked surprised. "Why?"

"Because that would be like a real race for Storm—he'd have to run his hardest. Maybe the allowance horses were too easy. But the only thing is . . ." Cindy didn't know how to say what she was thinking to Ashleigh.

"What?"

"I kind of think Storm will beat Mr. Wonderful at a half mile," Cindy said. She hoped Ashleigh wouldn't take that wrong, but Cindy was almost sure of it—if

Storm decided to give the work everything he had. "What if we cure Storm, but Mr. Wonderful gets depressed?"

"He won't. He's a seasoned racehorse, and he's not nearly as sensitive as Storm." Ashleigh took a deep breath. "All right, let's try it. But I hope you're right, Cindy, because if you're not—"

"Storm will lose on Sunday. He'll feel even worse," Cindy finished. "I know."

"Sammy was about to work Mr. Wonderful a half mile anyway," Ashleigh said.

Cindy nodded. She had seen the notation for a half-mile work on Mr. Wonderful's chart in the barn.

"Hey, Sammy!" Ashleigh called when Samantha rode Mr. Wonderful into earshot.

Ashleigh explained their plan, and Samantha nodded. "It's like we're having a match race," she joked.

Cindy's throat was dry as the two horses galloped off. This was Storm's last chance. *I hope I know what I'm doing,* she thought. *Maybe I should have just waited to see if Ashleigh would change her mind about scratching Storm and let him take his chances in the race.*

The two colts approached the half-mile marker, gaining speed. Cindy saw Ashleigh and Samantha crouch forward on the horses, asking for run.

Mr. Wonderful immediately shot into a fast gallop and drew off by a length. Cindy sucked in a sharp breath. "Please, Storm," she whispered. "Go after him!"

As if he had heard, the gray colt slowly pulled even with Mr. Wonderful. "Yes!" Cindy gasped. Mr. Wonderful was one of the best stakes horses in the country. If Storm kept pressing Mr. Wonderful even a little longer, Cindy knew Storm would have earned his way back into the race Sunday.

Suddenly Storm was blazing. A gray streak of speed, he opened up a length lead over Mr. Wonderful, then two lengths. Cindy almost stopped breathing.

Storm doesn't look the same horse he was a second ago! she thought. The two colts blistered by the finish with Storm ahead by a length. Mr. Wonderful had started to close, but he hadn't caught up in time.

Cindy noticed that almost all the riders on the track had pulled up their mounts to watch the short race. "I would have liked to bet on that one," commented a young trainer with short sandy hair. "I think I would have picked the wrong horse, though. I thought for sure Mr. Wonderful would win."

But Storm won! Cindy exulted. She still could hardly believe it.

Ashleigh and Samantha trotted back to the gap. "Wow!" Ashleigh called. "I think we've got a racehorse again!"

Cindy looked quickly at Mr. Wonderful to see how he was taking his defeat. The honey-colored colt was pulling vigorously at the reins, as if he would like to get going again. If the race had continued, Cindy

102

knew he probably would have won. She was glad Mr. Wonderful seemed to know that, too.

Storm was dancing proudly across the track, shivering with excitement.

"You were just great, boy!" Cindy praised. She walked across the track to collect the colt's reins. Storm bumped her urgently with his nose, as if to remind her again of his victory.

"Don't forget what we just did when we get to the race on Sunday, Storm," Ashleigh cautioned as she dismounted.

"He won't." Cindy lovingly patted the colt's shoulder. She was sure they were past every hurdle now.

"Go, Storm!" Cindy cheered, standing on tiptoe next to Mike in the stands. It was Sunday and the horses were approaching the gate for the Hutcheson. Cindy doubted if Storm could hear her—the horses were loading on the far side of the track. But she thought it would do him good if he did.

A few people in the reserved seating turned to smile at Cindy. Most of the boxes in the stands were filled with owners and other horsepeople, and they all knew that Storm was a Whitebrook horse.

Cindy was relieved that none of the horses from the Holy Bull were entered in the Hutcheson. She knew this was an entirely different race, at a different distance. But she thought Storm might have a bad reaction if he saw those horses again. "What do you think of the field?" Cindy asked Mike.

"This race is a Kentucky Derby prep for Smokin' Gun and Byyourleave," Mike said. "They're the four and six horses. Assuming the colts make a decent showing in this race, both trainers want to run them in the Fountain of Youth Stakes in three weeks. It's a race at one and one-sixteenth miles, and they'll try the colts then on two turns."

Cindy frowned. So many of the horses Storm would race against were headed for the Kentucky Derby in May. The Kentucky Derby was a mile and a quarter race, and so Storm wasn't a contender for that, but he still had to run against the best three-year-olds in the country.

"Sir Royale is going to give Storm a run for it today, too," Samantha said. "Like Storm, he's a winning sprinter. He set a track record for six furlongs at Turf Paradise in Phoenix."

"Yes, but the track was extremely fast." Ian squeezed Cindy's shoulders. "Don't worry—we think Storm's going to take the honors!"

"I do, too," Cindy said firmly. "Storm probably would have set the record at Turf Paradise if he'd run there that day."

A dark gray seagull flew gracefully under the stands, then floated over the track, moving out of the shade. The sun lit its wings, and in a burst of color the gull changed to light gray and white. *That's a good sign*, Cindy thought with a smile.

She felt oddly relaxed as Storm loaded into the gate, even though he was the last horse in the seven-horse field. Normally Cindy would be worried that the colt's position was so far to the outside. He had a long way to go through traffic to reach the rail, the shortest distance around the track. But Cindy was sure that today Storm was ready for any challenge.

The starting bell clanged shrilly as the gate flipped open and the horses surged into the race. Storm broke fast, and Ashleigh angled him toward the rail. Sir Royale and Byyourleave cut Storm off on his move to the rail, but Storm was on the lead by a nose!

"And it's Storm's Ransom, in and among horses," the announcer said. "Half a length back to Sir Royale, Byyourleave in third."

"The fast break, then straight to the lead is Storm's trademark style," Mike said excitedly. Cindy knew how much Mike loved sprinters. She was sure he wanted Storm to come back as a sprinter just as much as she did.

"Going right to the lead wasn't successful for Storm in the Holy Bull," Ian called over the crowd noise. "But that was a much longer race."

Cindy could see that Storm wasn't giving up an inch. The dark gray colt dug in, fighting to keep his lead. Cindy was afraid to look at the fractions on the board. She knew they were extremely fast. As in the Holy Bull, most of the horses couldn't keep up. The four other horses in the field were running another race ten lengths back.

"The field is turning for home," the announcer called. "And it's Storm's Ransom—but Sir Royale is charging up on the inside! Back two lengths from Sir Royale to Byyourleave, gaining with every stride!"

Cindy quickly focused her binoculars. She saw Ashleigh lean forward, crouching lower over Storm's neck. Storm responded to the challenge, again surging ahead of Sir Royale!

"Ashleigh had to ask Storm for more speed," Ian said. "If he gets shuffled to the back of the pack, this race is lost."

"He's got it!" Samantha said. "But I don't know if he can keep it up to the wire—the pace is absolutely blistering."

"Don't burn out, Storm!" Cindy cried, clenching her hands into fists.

"Whew, this is going to be close!" Mike shouted.

Sir Royale was gaining again on Storm. "Is Storm slowing down?" Cindy asked desperately.

"No, Sir Royale is going faster," Samantha said. "But they're coming down to the last furlong!"

If Storm can just hang on! Cindy thought frantically. As the horses moved into full view nearing the wire, Cindy could tell that the colt was in distress. His tail was flicking, and he was almost black from sweat.

Byyourleave and Sir Royale suddenly surged to within a length of Storm, one coming up on the inside and one on the outside. "No!" Cindy cried. "Hold them off, Storm!"

Storm refused to surrender the lead. Cindy could

see that he was holding the two other colts off—he was gaining! The wire flashed overhead and Storm had won by a length!

"He's back." Cindy brushed happy tears from her eyes. "He did so much!"

"Let's go tell him!" Samantha said with a laugh.

On the track Ashleigh and Sir Royale's jockey had already ridden their horses to the gap. "Nice one, Ashleigh—I admit Storm's fast," said Felipe Aragon, Sir Royale's jockey. Felipe had ridden Glory in many of his races.

Ashleigh smiled. "Thanks, Felipe. We sure had a good day."

Cindy ran to Storm, her heart pounding. She had seen from the stands that the colt was tired. But close up, he looked so exhausted, she was frightened. Every inch of him was soaked with sweat, and his nostrils showed red as he heaved in breaths. "Boy . . . are you okay?" she whispered. "You did so well—you're the bravest horse ever!"

The colt abruptly turned to look at her, and Cindy knew in an instant she didn't need to worry about him. Storm's eyes glittered with triumph. Carrying his neck and tail proudly, he pranced after Ashleigh toward the winner's circle.

Cindy and everyone from Whitebrook, including Beth holding Kevin, crowded around Storm for the winner's picture. Storm stood still as a statue in the winner's circle, as if he knew exactly why he was there. Looking proudly at her horse, Cindy wondered if someday he would be honored with a statue at one of the tracks, like some of the great horses of the past.

"Okay, let's get him back to the barn and take care of him," Mike said.

"He deserves the best!" Cindy reached for the colt's reins.

"They used to call Bold Ruler the Lord of Speed," Ashleigh said. Cindy knew that Ashleigh was referring to the sire of Secretariat, the great Triple Crown winner. "I think we've got a new Lord of Speed!"

"It sure looks that way," Cindy said, laughing with joy and relief as she hugged Storm's head. *I don't think I'll ever have to worry about him again*, she thought.

10

A FEW DAYS LATER CINDY AND CHAMPION LOOKED IN THE front door of the Reeses' house. The pink of dawn had just begun to glimmer in the east, and the first wakeful birds called quietly from the trees. "Ashleigh?" she said.

Cindy had gotten back from the Gulfstream track on Monday, after a big celebration with Storm on Sunday night. Cindy had brushed him, massaged him, and praised him a hundred different ways. Then she had made him a victory cake out of sweet feed, pushing carrots through the sticky grain. She had decided for Storm that he would like to share his cake with Mr. Wonderful and his other stable-mates.

Now that the problems with Storm seemed solved, Cindy wanted to dedicate herself to making Champion into a racehorse. The first step, she thought, was to do as Ashleigh had suggested—take

Champion everywhere with her. Cindy had begun the first morning she had been home from Gulfstream.

The big dark brown colt seemed to like his new routine. So far this morning Champion had watched Cindy eat breakfast, standing with her just outside the McLeans' cottage. The colt had gently sniffed at Cindy's plate of pancakes, then stood patiently. His scratch from running into the rail was completely healed, and Cindy hoped Champion was ready to turn over a new leaf.

Ashleigh came to the door of her house, holding Christina. Christina's nose was red, and she was whimpering.

"What's the matter?" Cindy asked with concern.

"Oh, she's just got a cold. She had a pretty miserable night," Ashleigh said. "I'll be ready in a second. Here comes Len—he's going to watch her while I go to the track with you."

"I'm glad you can come," Cindy said gratefully. Today she and Ashleigh planned to try Champion in the starting gate. Cindy didn't know exactly what to expect from the headstrong colt, but she was sure she would need Ashleigh's help.

Champion stretched his nose out to Christina, as if he were trying to make sense of the bundle of blankets and small red face.

Christina's hazel eyes widened. Then she smiled.

"That's the first time she's smiled in forty-eight hours," Ashleigh said tiredly. "Even if Champion won't go in the gate, Cindy, maybe we've found a vocation for him—comforting the sick."

Cindy nodded. Christina might have found a vocation, too, she thought—getting racehorses used to babies.

"Come to Uncle Len," Len said, clucking to the baby. Christina settled comfortably into his arms.

"I'll be back soon, Len," Ashleigh said. "Maybe very soon if Champion doesn't cooperate."

"He's behaved himself so far today," Cindy said hopefully. As if to underscore her words, Champion gave a yank on the reins. Cindy almost laughed at the alert expression on the colt's face. He seemed to be saying, What next?

Ashleigh shut the door to her house, and Cindy and Champion walked along the path with her to the track. The sun had risen above white and pink clouds, and the morning was cool and still. *It's such a nice morning to be out with the horses,* Cindy thought.

Then she saw her dad standing at the rail, watching Vic and Mark work Limitless Time and another two-year-old colt, Freedom's Ring. *Champion may cooperate about the gate, but I'm not sure Dad will!* she thought.

"Cindy, what are you doing with him?" Ian asked as Cindy approached the track with Champion.

Cindy hadn't ridden the colt since her fall a week ago, but she had saddled and bridled him for the gate lesson. "Ashleigh wants to try him in the gate."

"Are you going to sit on him for the gate work?" Ian didn't sound happy.

111

"Yes, but just for a few minutes. Ashleigh will be right there." Cindy tried to sound reassuring.

"Cindy, teaching a horse to go into the gate is very dangerous." Ian shook his head. "Champion could flip or crush you against the side."

"He wouldn't do that." Cindy knew the colt had a bad reputation for acting up, but she was sure he was too smart to go completely crazy on her.

Ian looked at the colt for a long moment, then at Cindy. "All right," he said with a sigh. "But be very careful, Cindy. And I'll be watching you. At the first sign of trouble, I want you to get off."

"Sure." Cindy quickly led Champion over to the gate before her dad could change his mind.

Ashleigh gave Cindy a leg into the saddle. "Okay, the first step is getting him to go right up to the gate," she said. "He should be used to seeing it since it's always parked right to the side of the track."

Cindy nodded. The practice gate had four stalls and was similar to an actual gate at races, with doors at the front and back. Cindy knew that it was critical to get the colt used to loading in the starting gate. Races could be lost on a bad break from the gate.

Champion balked just in front of the practice gate. The colt's ears were pricked, and he was snorting lightly.

"I know, that gate is weird looking," Cindy said sympathetically. "But you have to go in there, Champion. It's part of racing."

The colt slowly moved forward a few steps. Then he stopped and stared at the gate.

"Don't act up," Cindy said soothingly. "Dad's watching us. If you won't behave for me, somebody else is going to try. And I know you won't like that at all."

Champion eyed her. "Come on," Cindy urged.

The colt took a hesitant step forward. "That's right," Cindy said softly. "You always go with me. You came with me even when I was weaning you, remember?"

Wonder's Champion seemed to make up his mind. With a bob of his head he walked briskly into the gate. Ashleigh had left both the front and the back door open so that the colt wouldn't feel trapped.

"Walk Champion right back out. Then take him through a couple more times," Ashleigh said.

Without incident Cindy walked the colt in and out of the gate. "I think he's used to it," she said, patting Champion's sleek brown neck. The colt's eyes were bright and interested, but he definitely wasn't afraid.

"Let's try closing the front gate on him," Ashleigh said. "Then back him out." Cindy knew that Ashleigh wanted her to back Champion out of the gate so that he wouldn't learn to break slowly out the front.

Once again Cindy walked the colt into the gate. Ashleigh shut the front gate on them with a loud clang.

Champion trembled, bracing his legs. "It's okay," Cindy reassured him. "You've heard banging doors before."

The colt seemed to accept her explanation. With a little sigh, he dropped his head and stood calmly in the gate. Cindy backed him out.

"I'll shut both doors on him now," Ashleigh said after the colt had tried a few times with the front door shut. "But Cindy, watch out. The confinement's probably going to scare him."

"Got it." Cindy was thrilled at how well Champion was doing. But she knew that both doors closed would be the real test.

The front door clanged shut, then a moment later the back door. Champion snorted. The whites showed around his dark eyes as he looked back around at Cindy.

"I'm right here, boy," she said.

The colt shivered, looking around the close confines of the gate. "Easy, boy," Cindy said softly. "It's going to be okay. You believe me, don't you?"

Champion half reared. "Hang on. I'll open the back gate," Ashleigh said immediately.

"No, wait! Steady, boy," Cindy said urgently, putting a reassuring hand on the colt's sleek shoulder. "Trust me."

Cindy held her breath. If Champion tried to batter down the gate, his training might be set back for months.

The colt continued to look at her. Then he huffed out a sigh. After a firm stamp of his hoof, he stood still.

Moments later Ashleigh opened the door, and Cindy backed the colt out. "That was great!" she said happily. She looked quickly over at her dad. Ian was walking over to them. "You picked a very good time to behave, Champion," Cindy congratulated him.

"That's enough for today," Ashleigh said. "Most horses don't go in the gate that well the first time. Champion's doing beautifully, Cindy."

"Yes, he is," Ian agreed.

"Dad, can I try exercise-riding him again?" Cindy asked. After such a good performance, surely Champion deserved another chance to prove himself on the track, she thought.

Ian hesitated. *Say yes*, Cindy pleaded silently. *I just know it will work if I ride him now.*

Her dad shook his head. "Not yet, Cindy. Let's give him a little more time. If he keeps improving, I'll at least reconsider my decision. Good job, honey."

"It's not going to help much if Champion can go in the gate, but I can't take him around the track," Cindy complained as she and Ashleigh took Champion back to the barn.

"Ian was impressed with what he saw today. I think he'll change his mind," Ashleigh said reassuringly.

"Yes, but when?" Cindy sighed with frustration.

"What did you get for problem seven?" Heather asked Cindy the next Saturday. The girls were up in Cindy's bedroom, sharing her desk to do homework.

"The square root of x," Cindy answered.

Heather groaned.

"What's the matter?" Cindy looked over at her friend's paper. "You got that answer, too."

"It's not that. I just can't believe we're doing homework on Saturday afternoon! It's beautiful outside," Heather said.

"You know I'm waiting for Ashleigh to call and tell me how Mr. Wonderful came out of the Donn." Mr. Wonderful had won the major race that afternoon at Gulfstream by an unbelievable six lengths. Cindy had watched every second of the race on TV, cheering as loudly as if she were at the track.

"Do you think Ashleigh will call soon?" Heather pushed away her math book.

"Probably." Cindy nodded.

"I don't know if I even want to think about homework on the weekend," Heather said.

"I do." Cindy vigorously scribbled the answer to the problem.

"Why?" Heather dropped her head onto her hand.

"Because I have to miss more school to see Storm race, and my parents won't let me unless my grades are good. I can't go to Storm's next race—he'll be running in the Deputy Minister Handicap next weekend. But I want to go as early as possible for the Breeders' Cup Sprint Championship in March. Mike just entered Storm in that." Cindy added a column of figures and wrote the answer with a flourish.

"Cindy, it's Ashleigh on the phone," Beth called from downstairs.

"Great!" Cindy hurried to the hall phone. "Now I can hear every detail about the Donn."

"I guess you saw the race," Ashleigh's voice came over the phone. Cindy was having trouble hearing her. Cindy could tell that Ashleigh was still mobbed by the press and well-wishers.

"Yeah, it was incredible! Did Mr. Wonderful come out of it all right?"

"Just perfect," Ashleigh said. "We've already made the decision to send him out to California for the Santa Anita Handicap in March. He'll get a bonus if he wins that race, the Hollywood Gold Cup Handicap in June at Hollywood Park, and the Pacific Classic in August at Del Mar. Doesn't that sound fantastic?"

"You bet!" Cindy said excitedly.

A voice called out to Ashleigh on the other end of the line. "I've got to go—someone wants to interview Ian and me on TV," Ashleigh said. "See you soon, Cindy."

Cindy hung up the phone and returned to her room.

"Are we going outside now?" Heather asked hopefully.

"Just a minute—I have to make a phone call," Cindy said. She quickly looked in her mom's address book for the number at the Gulfstream track.

"What are you doing?" Heather asked.

"Calling my dad."

"Why? You just talked to Ashleigh." Heather sounded frustrated.

"I need to ask him if I can ride Champion again," Cindy said. She waited impatiently while the phone rang at the track. Finally she heard Mike's voice. "Hello?"

"Hi, Mike, it's Cindy. Is my dad around?" Cindy asked.

"No, he's still talking to the press."

"Oh," Cindy said slowly. "I was just wondering . . . well, I guess I could ask you. Can I try taking Champion around the track again?"

"It's fine with me," Mike replied. "I heard he did well in the gate a couple of days ago."

"Hey, Mike, you're on!" somebody called in the background.

"I've got to go, Cindy," Mike said. "You can take Champion out. But make sure Len is with you."

Cindy hung up the phone, grinning. *Perfect*, she thought. With just herself and Len around, she would have a relaxed setting to try riding the colt again.

Heather was staring at her. "That was Mike? Why didn't you ask your dad about riding Champion?"

"Because Dad was on TV, too," Cindy said evasively.

"No, really, Cindy."

Cindy bit her lip. "I was going to ask him, but now I'm glad I didn't. I'm not sure he'd let me ride Champion again."

"You're going to get in trouble when he finds out," Heather warned.

"I know." Cindy sighed. "But if I can just show

him real progress with Champion, maybe he'll let me keep riding him."

"I'll try to help you," Heather said. "Is there anything I can do?"

"Would you find Len and tell him we're taking Champion out? I'll get him out of the paddock."

"Sure," Heather said.

I shouldn't be doing this, Cindy thought guiltily as she walked to the front paddock. *But if I don't, Champion may never get his chance!*

"Champion!" Cindy called, leaning on the fence.

The dark chestnut colt's ears shot up. With a little whinny he walked energetically to the fence. Champion put his head over the gate and teasingly grabbed her shirt with his teeth. He let it go and tossed his head.

Cindy's heart lifted at his beauty. "Come on," she said, clipping a lead line to the colt's halter. "I know you're going to do just fine today."

"I'm glad this boy is finally getting out again," Len said as Cindy led Champion into the barn and put him in crossties. "I think he's ready."

"I do, too!" Cindy knew trying the colt again could be dangerous, but she felt thrilled at the prospect.

With Heather and Len's help she gave the colt a quick brushing. "I've never seen you ride him," Heather said.

"Well, you're in for a treat if he behaves." Cindy adjusted the cinch of the saddle and took Champion out of the barn.

Len gave her a leg up and Cindy sat deep in the saddle, checking the length of her stirrups. "I don't suppose I have to tell you to watch him out there," Len said.

Cindy nodded. She knew that better than anyone.

As she walked the colt to the track the wind picked up, scattering dry leaves and small branches across the stable yard. *I wish stuff wouldn't blow around*, Cindy thought. *Champion will be even more likely to act up.* She pushed away her nervousness. This session had to go well.

Champion stopped at the gap and pricked his ears. "Take a good look," Cindy urged. "I don't want you spooking at anything."

The colt gazed at the deserted track for a long time. Then he whinnied loudly and stretched his neck toward the track.

"Okay, let's get out there." Cindy patted his neck.

"Just trot him," Len said, coming up beside her. "Don't let him get away from you, Cindy. He hasn't been galloped in months, except—"

"When he ran away with me," Cindy finished. "I'll watch him."

Cindy moved the colt out at a brisk walk. The breeze blew back Cindy's hair and ruffled Champion's thick mane. *Spring's really coming*, she thought.

Champion danced lightly across the dirt, pulling on the reins and asking for his head. But his ears were flicked back. He was waiting for her instructions, Cindy realized. That was different. She wondered if their walks had helped to focus his attention on her.

"Let's try a trot," Cindy said. "But that's *all* we're going to do, Champion. Trot does not mean gallop. Sometimes you don't seem to understand that."

Cindy carefully eased the colt into the faster pace. Champion had a quick spring in his strides and a floating smoothness to his gait. Despite herself Cindy unclenched her hands, relaxing into the beautiful trot. *There's something special about the way he moves*, she said to herself. *I've always thought that, but now I'm sure.*

The wind caught a small dead branch, twirling it near the colt's feet. Champion jumped away from the branch. Arching his neck, he broke into a fast trot.

"No, Champion!" Cindy cried, pulling back on the reins. Champion would always be a thousand times stronger than she was. He just had to listen to her!

The colt snorted again and eyed the branch. He dropped his pace.

"That's the way," Cindy praised him breathlessly. Champion continued around the track at a brisk trot, staying just the right distance from the rail. He acted as if he had exercised perfectly on the track his entire life.

Cindy pulled him up at the gap. "Wow, I think that's the first time you ever got all the way around the track without running away! You were wonderful, boy!"

"Good job, Champion," Heather agreed.

121

"One more time around at a trot," Len said. "Very good, Cindy. You're handling him well."

Cindy gathered the reins, her face flushed with pleasure at the praise and the colt's success. She only hoped her dad wouldn't be too angry with her. *But he'll understand,* she told herself. *I just know I'm right to do this.*

"Heather, guess what?" A week later Cindy darted through the crowded hall at school to reach her friend. "I tried to call you all yesterday. Storm won the Deputy Minister Handicap!"

"That's so great!" Heather beamed. "Too bad you couldn't be there."

"Well, I don't think I have to be anymore." Cindy leaned against a row of lockers, trying to catch her breath. "Storm won the race by five lengths. It's really Champion who needs me now."

Heather dropped her voice, even though none of the other kids rushing through the halls were paying them any attention. "How's Champion doing?"

"Really well. I've ridden him twice this week." Cindy shifted her books to her right arm. The left one still hurt sometimes from her fall off Champion, but she never told anyone. "I'm getting really nervous, though, about what Dad's going to say. Everyone but him knows I've been riding Champion."

"How did that happen?" Heather looked puzzled.

"Well, Mike and Len know I'm riding Champion, of course. And Mike must have told Ashleigh, because she talked to Len about it. Mike was home a couple of days ago, and he thought Champion looked fine—the riding I've been doing hasn't stressed his legs."

"He couldn't look better," Heather agreed.

"I think so, too. But the problem is—" Cindy hesitated. "Dad's coming home soon. Then *he's* going to find out that I've been riding Champion."

"Why didn't Ashleigh or Mike tell him?"

Cindy sighed deeply. "I think they did tell him Champion was back in training, but they didn't tell him I was riding. Dad must think Mark or Vic is exercising Champion."

"Are you going to be in a lot of trouble when your dad finds out?" Heather frowned.

"I don't know. Maybe not, if Champion keeps doing well. But if I'm in even a little trouble, I'm afraid Dad won't let me go to Storm's next race in a month. I just can't let that happen—it's a big race, the Breeders' Cup Sprint Championship at Gulfstream."

"Maybe your dad will understand," Heather said. But she looked worried, too.

11

ON SUNDAY A WEEK LATER CINDY AND HEATHER LED Wonder's Champion to the training track for his morning exercise. "You really are big for a two-year-old," Cindy told the colt as she mounted up. "Even though you're young to be two." Champion had turned officially two on January 1, as all Thoroughbreds did, but his real birthday was in early May. The colt would probably run in his first race sometime that summer—if all went well, Cindy thought. He had been improving rapidly since she had begun riding him again.

Cindy gulped. She wasn't at all sure things would continue to go well. For one thing, Ian had returned home last night.

Champion pulled energetically on the reins. The morning sun glinted off his burnished brown coat and clean white stockings. He occasionally bumped Cindy with his nose, as if to hurry her to the track. Clearly he didn't share Cindy's nervousness.

"I'm glad you're here," Cindy said to Heather. Heather had spent the night. "Ashleigh wants me to take Champion around. But Dad's home—"

"So he's going to find out you've been riding Champion." Heather shook her head.

"Yeah." Cindy drew a deep breath.

Cindy tried to stay calm as they approached the track. She remembered how years ago she had trained Glory without permission, then tried to show off his racing talent for her dad. Cindy had been so nervous, she had almost fallen off. Samantha had then ridden Glory, taking over for Cindy. But Cindy doubted if Champion would go well for anyone but her.

Cindy gripped the colt's reins with determination. This time she wouldn't let her horse down.

To her relief, Cindy saw that Ian wasn't at the track. *Maybe he won't find out today after all,* she thought.

"Oh, Cindy," Ashleigh called from the rail. "Ian will be up in a minute. I'll bet he can't wait to see Champion's progress."

Cindy smiled weakly, but her stomach lurched. *I'm going to be in so much trouble when Dad sees me riding, no matter how well Champion goes!* she thought. But she couldn't back out now.

Mike gave her a leg up into the saddle. As Cindy gathered her reins she saw that Ashleigh, Mike, and Samantha were all watching.

Just forget about them, she ordered herself. *You've got a job to do.* "Come on, Champion," she said confidently. "Let's get out there."

Cindy kept the colt at a walk as they circled the first half of the track. Wonder's Champion obeyed every command with easy familiarity, his long strides precise and graceful. Cindy's spirits soared. She put the colt into a trot and rode back by the gap. Again he minded perfectly.

"Excellent, Cindy." Cindy could hear the warm approval in Ashleigh's voice. "Now try him at a very short gallop. And I mean short—just a couple of strides. He doesn't have enough miles at a trot to ask him for more than that. But you're so light, it's almost as if he's galloping in the pasture."

"Can you do it?" Mike asked.

Cindy saw Ian emerge from the stallion barn and begin walking toward the track. "Sure." Cindy turned the colt, thankful for his swift, light responsiveness. *I've got to show Dad something good!* she thought. *If I'm going to get in trouble, it might as well be over a real ride, not just sitting on Champion.*

Cindy trotted the colt all the way around the track, timing the gallop to take place right in front of the gap. She saw her dad step onto the track as if he would stop them.

Now! Cindy crouched forward, cueing the colt for a gallop. He broke into the faster gait, but his movements were jerky. Suddenly she felt him lunge forward, trying to go into a dead run. Cindy pulled sharply on the reins. "Do this right!" Cindy whispered. "Please. I know you can, Champion."

The colt settled into a smooth gallop, his strides

clean and steady. "Yes!" Cindy laughed in triumph. She could feel the controlled power of the colt beneath her. The small movements of his head and neck told her that he was listening for her commands.

But Champion was clearly having a glorious time, too. The colt joyously bounded across the track, head high, mane and tail fanning out behind him. He seemed to have finally put together his intelligence and strength, and his love of running and of her, Cindy thought in wonder.

She quickly pulled the colt down to a trot. Champion was high stepping and yanking on the reins, and his eyes glittered. "You know just how well you did, don't you?" she asked, posting back to the gap. "Now everyone is going to know just how much talent you have."

"Wow, Cindy!" Heather called. Cindy smiled at her friend.

Ian was scowling at her. "Cindy, I'm not at all happy about what you've done," he said. "You deliberately disobeyed me, and you could have been seriously injured. What I should do is forbid you to ride him ever again."

"I'm sorry." Cindy hung her head. *I should have known Dad would say that!* she thought miserably. *I've just made things worse for Champion.* She wondered what else her father would do to punish her. He might not let her be around the horses at all.

"But I've seen today that Champion has ability and that he can be controlled," Ian continued.

Cindy looked up in surprise. She hadn't expected praise.

"You've clearly figured out how to handle him, and I don't think it would be fair to the horse if you didn't ride him," Ian said. "So I want you to continue riding—but under close supervision, not behind anyone's back."

I can't believe it! Cindy stared at her father, then ran to him to give him a big hug. "Thanks so much, Dad! You won't regret it!"

"You may, though." Ian returned her hug. "You're on extra stall duty for two weeks. I want you to clean out ten stalls instead of five every morning. That will probably leave you time to ride only Champion."

"Okay!" Cindy said happily, throwing her arms around Champion's neck. *I'd clean out every barn in Kentucky for him,* she thought. *He's worth it.*

Two weeks later Cindy watched Mr. Wonderful win the Santa Anita Handicap on TV with her family and Max and Heather. "I can't believe it!" Cindy turned to Heather, her eyes shining. "Mr. Wonderful has three consecutive stakes wins!"

"Whitebrook does it again," Max agreed. "That's fantastic, Cindy."

"Isn't it?" Cindy said. She loaded another chip with Beth's delicious avocado dip. Chewing, Cindy thought about Ashleigh's brilliant strategy with Mr.

Wonderful in the mile and a quarter race. Mr. Wonderful had come from behind at the quarter pole and taken the lead, skimming the rail but with just enough room. Under Ashleigh's guidance the colt had a dream trip in the race.

The telephone rang. "I'll get it," Beth called over the noise of the celebration.

"So what's next for Mr. Wonderful?" Max asked Cindy.

"The Hollywood Gold Cup this summer," Cindy answered. "If he comes out of the race okay."

"I see," Beth said over the phone. Cindy glanced at Beth and saw that her face was grave. "Yes, of course I'll tell Ian."

"What's the matter?" Cindy asked when Beth had hung up.

"That was Tim Hevron over at Hillsdale Stables," Beth said quietly. "The first case of equine infectious anemia this year was just diagnosed in a horse near Louisville."

Cindy gasped. A chill ran down her arms, and the cake and chips she had just eaten churned in her stomach. "Oh no!"

"Cindy, don't panic yet," Beth said gently. "It's only one horse, and Louisville is almost a hundred miles from Whitebrook."

Cindy sat slowly down in a chair. Cold fear gripped her heart. *Not again,* she thought. *Oh, please, not again!* Cindy could hardly bear the thought of another spring, summer, and fall of fear about the horses' lives. Louisville might be a long way from Whitebrook, but the party was over for her anyway.

That night Cindy could hardly sleep, imagining that an epidemic would sweep over Whitebrook and kill all the horses. But as the days passed, gradually her fears died away. No more cases of equine infectious anemia were reported, and her thoughts turned to Storm's race in the Breeders' Cup Sprint Championship. Cindy would be on spring break most of the week of March 15, the date of the race.

Cindy had at first feared her father wouldn't let her go to the race because she had ridden Champion without his permission. But he hadn't said anything about it, and soon Cindy realized that everyone was assuming she would go.

Two days before the race Cindy began packing her bag. She would leave for Gulfstream the next morning by herself. Though she would miss having someone to talk to on the plane, she was excited at the prospect of traveling alone.

Samantha looked in the doorway to Cindy's bedroom. "Are you about ready for your trip?" she asked.

"Almost." Cindy always packed light to go to the track. She had put a nice outfit in her suitcase for race day, but otherwise she was just taking T-shirts and jeans. She figured the horses didn't care how she looked.

"Well, have fun." Samantha came inside the room and sat on Cindy's bed.

"Are you sure you won't change your mind about going?" Cindy asked. She loved traveling with her older sister.

"No, I really think I should stay here and work with Limitless Time," Samantha said. Cindy knew that the two-year-old son of Fleet Goddess was showing real promise. Samantha had always had a special relationship with Fleet Goddess, the first Thoroughbred she had ridden at Whitebrook. Now she seemed to love Limitless Time just as much. "But I'll be thinking about you," Samantha added. "Don't forget to call as soon as you can after the race."

"I won't." Cindy smiled.

Samantha got up. "Good luck," she said.

"I don't even know if we'll need it." Cindy snapped her suitcase shut.

Samantha hesitated in the doorway. "You always need good luck in a race," she said quietly.

The next evening Cindy almost flew across the Gulfstream backstretch toward the Whitebrook shedrow. She hadn't seen Storm in over a month, and she could hardly wait to be with the gray colt again. Fond as Cindy had become of Wonder's Champion, the younger colt didn't have the same place in her heart as Storm.

In the barn aisle Mike, Len, and Ashleigh were sitting in lawn chairs, reading racing papers. "Hi, Cindy!" Ashleigh waved and smiled.

131

"Hi." Cindy smiled back. It always felt so good to see everyone in the group again.

Storm abruptly poked his head out of his stall. Whickering repeatedly, he hopped up and down on his front feet. "Oh, I know—I've missed you, too!" Cindy said, kissing his soft muzzle.

Storm stood very still and sniffed her shirt. "Yes, it's really me," she assured him.

The colt took a final long sniff, then eagerly bobbed his head, as if to say, Well, let's do something!

"I think I'll take him for a walk," Cindy said.

"You should—it's a lovely evening," Ashleigh agreed.

Outside the barn the tropical sun was setting in a dramatic burst of bronze, cinnabar, and gold. Slender palm trees were silhouetted against the sky, their fronds bent by a soft breeze. Cindy could hardly believe how beautiful the evening was.

Storm waited quietly while she took her fill of looking at the sunset. Now that they were back together, he seemed content just being near her.

Cindy's heart filled with love for her horse. "I'm so glad I'm here with you again, Storm," she murmured. "You're a wonderful boy, do you know that?" Storm dropped his head into her arms contentedly.

A movement in the next shedrow over caught Cindy's eye. Sherri's Matchmaker and Sky Beauty, two other horses Cindy knew would be running in the Breeders' Cup Sprint Championship, were following their grooms outside to graze. Both horses were eagerly tugging at the lead ropes, trying to get to the grass.

"I've seen two of the main contenders in your race," Cindy said to Storm. "They're beautiful horses, but neither of them can compare to you. What do you think? Will you win tomorrow?"

The gray colt nudged her hands affectionately, as if to say that she shouldn't worry about a thing.

"Storm, please don't fall!" Cindy stared in horror at the track the next afternoon, and her hands flew to her mouth. Storm was staggering and trying to regain his balance. The colt had tripped barely a stride out of the gate in the Breeders' Cup Sprint Championship. The five other horses in the field surged around him.

"Hang on, Ashleigh!" Mike said. His jaw was clenched.

"She will." Beth gripped Cindy's shoulder.

In an instant Cindy saw that Ashleigh had anticipated most of the colt's movements in the misstep. She had leaned back when the colt went almost to his knees and held on tight. Gripping his mane, she urged him up to his feet again. In an instant Storm found his balance and roared after the rest of the field.

"Oh, thank goodness!" Cindy cried. But Storm was trailing by ten lengths in a seven-furlong race. He might be out of contention already.

"Sky Beauty is moving comfortably on the lead,

with Dancer's Dream up close second," the announcer called. "Three lengths back to Sherri's Matchmaker; Winner Take All in fourth and Cat's Meow in fifth. Storm's Ransom is running well behind the rest of the field."

"Storm doesn't deserve this!" Cindy pounded the rail in front of her in frustration. Storm had overcome so much to get to this race. She couldn't accept that it had all been for nothing. *If he loses again, he'll feel terrible!* she thought.

Cindy glanced at the board. The fractions were faster than they had been in the Holy Bull, where Storm had come out of the race exhausted. He would have to run even faster to catch the field here.

"It's too soon to give up," Ian said reassuringly.

Cindy saw that Storm had no intention of giving up. Hugging the rail as the field shot into the turn, he was gaining ground with every stride. He passed Winner Take All and Cat's Meow in a single bound. But all three frontrunners were squarely in front of Storm, running almost neck and neck.

"Storm's blocked!" Mike shook his head. "I just don't think he has the stamina to swing three wide and take them!"

Cindy sat down in frustration, then jumped back up again with nervous excitement. What else could go wrong in this race?

But Storm was digging in, pressing the pace with every stride. Suddenly he swung out three wide.

"There goes Storm's Ransom!" the announcer

cried. "He's full of run. But he still has a lot to do with just a furlong to the wire!"

Cindy almost stopped breathing. Storm roared around Dancer's Dream and Sherri's Matchmaker. Now only Sky Beauty was in front of him.

"Come on, boy! You can do it," Cindy screeched. She knew the colt must be exhausted, but he had so much courage!

At the sixteenth pole Storm found another gear and put away Sky Beauty. Driving hard, he pounded for the finish.

"Hang on, Storm. Go!" Cindy could hear the other members of the Whitebrook group calling their support.

"And it's Storm's Ransom, getting up in the final strides. He wins it by two lengths," the announcer said.

Cindy hugged her mother hard. "Wow, what a horse!" Beth said happily.

"I know—isn't he amazing?" Cindy was all smiles. "I wonder how fast he would have gone if he'd had a perfect trip?"

In the winner's circle a breeze fluttered Storm's silver mane and tail as Cindy held the colt for the winning photograph. Glittering like solid metal in the Florida sun, Storm looked relaxed and proud. His coat was soaked with sweat, but his neck was arched and his eyes bright. Storm was tired, Cindy thought, but not the way he had been after his defeat in the Holy Bull. With his elegant head and sweeping, beautiful lines, he seemed to Cindy the picture of what a superb Thoroughbred should be.

Cindy smiled as the photographers' cameras clicked, capturing the happy colt, the smiling group from Whitebrook, and the applauding crowd. "You're such a good boy, Storm," Cindy said softly, pressing her cheek to his gray muzzle. She knew she would remember this wonderful day forever.

12

CINDY OPENED THE DOOR OF THE TRAILER AND EASED Storm backward onto the ground at Whitebrook. "Isn't it great to be home?" she asked.

Smiling, Cindy sniffed the fresh air. Spring had come early on the farm this year. It was only the middle of March, but the buds were bursting on the trees, and the grass in the paddock shimmered emerald green.

Storm whickered throatily, as if he fully agreed. Looking him over, Cindy saw that she had work to do again. Storm had lost weight after the race three days ago, and his coat wasn't as shiny as before. *Well, that's just the way he is*, she decided. *Storm gets stressed out after every race. It isn't anything I have to worry about—I just have to deal with it.*

The colt leaned lovingly against Cindy, as if he knew that she would take care of him. Cindy closed her eyes and let the sun warm them, relaxing them both. "You'll get a rest now," she murmured. "You've certainly earned it."

Over the next few weeks Cindy exercised Wonder's Champion most mornings, but after school she walked Storm along the lanes to condition him. Cindy loved the long walks with her horse. Delicate white, purple, and gold spring flowers bloomed at the edge of the lane, and the trees were feathered with young leaves. Small songbirds perched on the feeders or in nearby trees and sang sweetly as Cindy and the big gray colt passed.

After a morning of exercising Champion, Cindy was ready in the afternoon for Storm's gentle company. Champion's training was going more smoothly these days, but the colt still had a trying personality. Some mornings he promptly settled down and walked, trotted, and galloped exactly the way Cindy told him to. Other days he was utterly impossible and would even resist her commands to walk, throwing up his head, backing, or trying to suddenly bolt up the track.

One afternoon after an especially rough session with Champion she brought him back to the barn, flexing her sore fingers. But the colt wouldn't go near his stall. He lifted on his hind legs and let out a little squeal. Cindy almost laughed at the contrary expression in his dark eyes.

"You just enjoy being bad," she said. "But I don't have time for this, Champion. You have to go into the barn." She gave a hard tug on his lead rope.

Suddenly Champion strode into the barn, dragging Cindy behind him. "Well, that's not exactly how I imagined it, but okay," Cindy said, and unlatched his stall door.

I think I'll go see Glory and Storm for a minute, she thought, shutting Champion inside. Glory and Storm had already been turned out to graze. Cindy turned to go, ignoring the indignant look the chestnut colt was giving her over the half door.

As she passed the stable office Cindy looked in at the sound of voices. Mike and her dad were sitting at the desk.

"Hi, Cindy," Mike said. "We were just talking about Storm."

"He looks good these days," Ian added. "You've worked more magic on him, honey. We'll probably enter him in a sprint at Churchill Downs in early May."

"Great!" Cindy beamed. "Then I should start riding him again to get him ready, right?"

Ian nodded. "Why don't you take him out on the trails today after school? If Max wants to come along, he could ride the quarter horse we're boarding for his mom. The horse needs exercise, and Dr. Smith mentioned that Max might ride him over here."

Cindy knew that Whitebrook didn't train quarter horses, but Dr. Smith had left the horse, just off the quarter horse racetracks, at Whitebrook while she was out of town at a conference. Max was staying with his grandmother.

"I'll tell Max at school today." Cindy was already planning where they would go. They could do a good warm-up trot along the lanes, then ride through the woods to their favorite meadow.

Cindy wanted to give Storm some real exercise. Now that her dad and Mike were planning to race the colt, she knew it was time to get serious about his training again.

This is Daly Bar Dun," Max said after school that afternoon. He had just crosstied the gelding in the training barn aisle at Whitebrook.

Cindy walked over to examine the gorgeous dun quarter horse. Daly Bar Dun had a short black mane and tail, and a black dorsal stripe ran along his back from his withers to his tail. "He doesn't look like a racehorse to me," Cindy admitted. "He seems too heavy to move." But Cindy admired the quarter horse's broad chest and bunchy shoulder muscles. Daly Bar Dun looked like a tank.

"Believe me, he's fast," Max assured her.

"Oh, Cindy." Ian walked down the aisle toward them. "Sammy's going to go with you on Chips."

"How come?" Cindy was surprised. She and Samantha often rode together, but not when Cindy already had a companion. The rule at Whitebrook was that no one rode alone.

"She'll ride along just to make sure things go all right," Ian said. "Daly only got here yesterday, and he may still be wound up."

"Sure." Cindy nodded.

"Keep the horses at a walk and trot," Ian added. "I know you and Max are good riders. Just don't do anything reckless."

"We won't," Cindy said. She knew that she had to be careful with Storm—he was extremely valuable.

"Are you guys ready?" Samantha called from outside the barn.

"Almost." Cindy bridled Storm, checked the saddle girth for the last time, and led him out of the barn. Storm walked quickly after her, shaking his head spiritedly. "It's been a while since somebody rode you, hasn't it?" Cindy smiled. "This will be a lot of fun."

Samantha was already mounted on Chips. The gentle Appaloosa calmly sniffed the newcomer and touched noses with Storm. "It looks like more rain," Samantha said. "We'd better get going."

Cindy looked at the sky. Fast-moving, low gray clouds were moving in, and the air was damp and chilly. "Yeah, I hope we don't get caught out there."

As they rode toward the woods the clouds swept lower, almost skimming the treetops, and a fine mist beaded in Cindy's blond hair. "Should we go back?" Max asked.

"Let's not unless it rains harder," Cindy said. "The horses love the cool temperatures." Storm was prancing eagerly forward, as if he could hardly wait to find out what was around every turn of the trail. Even gentle Chips was walking briskly, stopping only occasionally to sample the fresh leaves on a bush or tree.

"It's not really cold," Samantha agreed.

Cindy watched Max's quarter horse nimbly pick his way around fallen brush. "Daly doesn't seem excited, even though all this is new to him," Cindy remarked. "If he's from the Southwest, he's not even used to trees, is he? Isn't he a desert horse?"

Max laughed. "They have trees in the Southwest—I've been there. But yeah, Daly's used to sand and wide-open spaces."

"I bet he likes it here," Cindy said.

"He seems to—quarter horses are pretty laid back," Max replied. "But I guess Daly isn't laid back on the track."

A gray squirrel chattered at them from the top of a tree, and Cindy tipped back her head to watch him. The soft mist felt cool and good on her face.

The squirrel jumped to a lower branch. To Cindy's surprise, the squirrel missed and tumbled through the air. It landed right at Daly Bar Dun's feet.

The quarter horse snorted sharply and stepped away, trying to see the squirrel. The small animal was lying still and seemed dazed.

"Poor little guy," Cindy said. Suddenly the squirrel leapt to its feet and chattered angrily. Daly Bar Dun trembled from head to tail.

"What's wrong with Daly?" Cindy asked, but before the words were even out of her mouth, Daly

Bar Dun had taken off like a rocket. Fortunately he barely missed the angry squirrel with his hooves.

A second later Cindy realized she should have minded her own business. Storm roared in full pursuit after Daly Bar Dun. "Storm, stop!" Cindy grabbed the saddle cantle with one hand and Storm's mane with the other as she fought to stay in the saddle. *Do* not *fall!* she ordered herself. If Storm got loose, he could be injured. Cindy could hear Samantha and Chips pounding after her, but Chips was no match for Storm.

Slowly Cindy shifted her weight until she was balanced on the colt's back again. To her horror, Storm was taking little jumps over tree branches. He wasn't trained at all as a jumper! What if he tripped?

They burst from the woods, and Storm slowed a fraction. Cindy pulled hard on the reins, rhythmically applying pressure to his mouth. Just ahead she saw Max and Daly Bar Dun. The gelding also seemed to have slowed.

Good, Max has Daly under control! Cindy barely had time to think before Storm saw the other horse. In an instant he leapt back into a racing gallop and thundered by the quarter horse.

The next second Daly Bar Dun raced after them, trying to catch Storm. Cindy realized that Max must have thought he had his horse under control, too.

"Circle them when you get to the meadow!" Samantha called. Her voice seemed far away. "But don't run into each other!"

143

Cindy didn't dare to take her attention away from Storm to shout a reply. *Good plan, Sammy,* she thought tensely. The next moment Cindy almost cried out as Daly Bar Dun roared up on Storm's flank.

"Keep your distance!" she screamed to Max. "Don't hit us!"

"I'm trying!" Max yelled back. Both Daly Bar Dun and Storm were trained racehorses, Cindy thought rapidly. They should know not to run into each other.

What if Storm smashes into a tree or falls in a rabbit or groundhog hole? she thought as the ground flew by. But the meadow was just ahead to her right. If she could only guide Storm there, she might be able to get him back under control without injuring him.

"I'm turning Storm now!" she called to Max. She pulled hard on Storm, praying he wouldn't slip and fall on the damp ground.

Like circus horses, Storm and Daly Bar Dun galloped in a large circle around the meadow. Cindy almost cried with relief when she felt Storm's pace drop off a notch. Within seconds she and Max had the horses back into a trot. Cindy stopped Storm at the back of the meadow.

Max stared at her, his face pale. "That was close," he said.

"Too close," Cindy said. She quickly dismounted and walked around Storm. She was almost afraid to look at him. *What if we hurt them?* she thought. Cindy knew she should have been better prepared. Storm hadn't been ridden in a couple of weeks, and he was with a strange racehorse. No wonder they had taken off.

"Is he okay?" Max asked.

"I think so." Miraculously Storm didn't seem to have a scratch on him. The gray colt was watching Cindy calmly, breathing easily.

"Storm, you worried me so much." Cindy rested her forehead against the colt's neck. "How's Daly?" she asked Max.

"Fine, I think." Max shook his head. "Boy, were we lucky."

"What happened?" Samantha pulled up Chips next to them. She looked worried and upset.

"I guess Daly never saw a squirrel before." Cindy's voice still shook. She remounted Storm, almost slipping down the colt's side. Her legs still felt rubbery.

"Are you both okay to ride back?" Samantha asked. "We could just lead the horses. Or I'll trade you—one of you can ride Chips."

"I think Storm's settled down now," Cindy said. The colt was responding easily to her hands. He was high stepping and snorting and acting altogether pleased with himself. *He knows he won a race*, Cindy thought.

"Daly won't do that again," Max said. "The squirrel just startled him since it dropped down out of a tree and got right under his feet."

Samantha groaned. "I'm starting to feel like Dad! Don't worry me like that again, you guys. I just hope the horses are really okay and they don't have an injury that shows up later."

"Me too." Cindy felt almost sick at the thought of it. "We're really sorry, Sammy."

Samantha managed a weak smile. "Well, I guess you have to learn what not to do. But I don't want you to get killed in the process."

On the way home Samantha rode ahead of them. Cindy wondered if her older sister thought Storm and Daly would race again.

"Hey, Cindy," Max said softly. "Didn't the horses run about a quarter mile once we got out of the woods?"

Cindy tried to think. She knew the lanes well, but their wild ride was still mostly a blur. "I guess so," she said at last. "Why?"

"Well, Storm beat Daly Bar Dun."

"So? Storm's fast." Cindy could feel her heart slowing to its normal rate. She sighed, feeling the tension ease out of her shoulders.

"So Daly is a star racehorse, too. My mom said he's one of the fastest horses in the Southwest—at a quarter mile. He's set two track records."

"Oh." Cindy was startled. She remembered that quarter horses were blindingly fast at short distances. And if this quarter horse was as fast as Max said . . .

She looked at Storm, elegantly picking his way around fallen logs and brush as they made their way back through the woods. For the first time she wondered just how fast he had been going.

146

You were really blazing, she thought, running her hand along Storm's gray withers. *And you beat a quarter horse at a quarter mile. Maybe no horse has ever been as fast as you.*

13

"Let's go, Storm!" Cindy called cheerfully as she walked into the barn on Friday morning. "Today we're going out on the track!" After a week of trail work Mike, Ian, and Ashleigh thought the colt was ready to return to galloping on the track.

Storm wasn't looking out of his stall for her the way he usually was. *He must be sleeping in,* Cindy thought. But she walked faster. Storm might have colicked and gone down.

Just as Cindy reached Storm's stall the colt put his head over the half door. "There you are!" Cindy said with relief. "You scared me."

The gray colt stepped closer to the door and dropped his head into her arms. "Come on, boy," Cindy said. "We've got work to do." Then she noticed that the colt's nose was running a little.

"Dad? Could you come here for a minute?" Cindy tried to keep the fear out of her voice.

She heard her dad's footsteps in the aisle, then Ian stood beside her. "What is it, sweetie?"

"Storm's sick." Now that Cindy looked closely at the colt, she could see that he really wasn't feeling well. He seemed listless and tired. Storm's head was heavy in her arms. She could tell he didn't really want to hold it up by himself.

Cindy felt her stomach knot up with dread. *What if Storm's really sick?* she thought. Cindy shook her head fiercely. *Don't be silly,* she told herself. *Horses get colds and the flu just like people. That's all it is.*

Ian examined the colt, frowning. "I don't like the looks of this. I'm going to call Dr. Smith."

Cindy felt her throat close over. "I'm staying with him."

"Cindy, go to school. It's not time to press the panic button yet," Ian said gently. "Storm's definitely sick, but he's not in too much discomfort."

Cindy knew there was no way she could talk her dad into letting her miss school without an important reason. In a way she was glad he wanted her to go. If he thought Storm was very sick, he would want her to stay home.

Cindy rubbed Storm's neck, and the colt leaned gratefully into her caress the way he always did. "Get better," she whispered. "I'll be back as soon as I can."

She walked slowly up to the house. Glory's distant whinny rang out from one of the back paddocks, but otherwise the farm was quiet.

A light fog, tinged pink by the rising sun,

wreathed the barns. Even the grass was pinkish in the early light. Whitebrook seemed the same as always, but Storm might be very sick. *Please let him be okay,* Cindy prayed. *And please, please don't let the other horses get sick.*

Cindy went through her morning classes in a daze of worry. She couldn't take her mind off Storm for more than a few seconds. Luckily none of Cindy's teachers called on her in class. She knew she wouldn't be able to answer the simplest question about English, math, or Spanish.

At lunch Cindy tried to eat, but every bite of her sandwich stuck in her throat.

"Our English assignment is so hard," Sharon said. "How will I have time to write a five-page composition by next Tuesday? And Mrs. Ellerton marks every little comma that's wrong."

"I bet Cindy's already got it done." Laura touched Cindy's shoulder. "Right?"

"What?" Cindy tried to focus on what Laura was saying.

Heather looked across the table at Cindy, her blue eyes full of sympathy. The minute Cindy had gotten to school that morning, she had told her best friend that Storm was sick. Heather had promised to come over to Whitebrook after school and see if there was anything she could do to help.

"What's the matter, Cindy?" Melissa poked the food on her tray with a fork. "You aren't eating, but

150

your lunch sure looks better than this gunk I just got from the lunch line. Want to trade?"

Max started to laugh, then he looked at Cindy. His expression abruptly changed to a frown. "What's up, Cindy?" he asked.

"Storm's sick," Cindy said quietly. She dropped her sandwich on her plate. Maybe if she told her friends that she had a sick horse, they would understand that she just needed to be left alone.

"Is he very sick or does he just have a cold or something?" Sharon asked with concern.

"Just a cold, I think." Cindy pushed away her lunch. "He has a runny nose and he's kind of tired."

"I hope he doesn't have equine infectious anemia," Melissa said. "This morning my dad was at Pine Shadows Farm near Versailles, and one of the horses there had just gotten sick with it. Since equine infectious anemia is incurable, the horses were going to be put down almost on the spot."

"Melissa," Heather scolded. "That's not going to make Cindy feel better."

Cindy jumped up and stuffed her sandwich into her lunch bag. *I have to get out of here*, she thought. If she stayed one more minute, she knew she was going to be sick to her stomach.

"Cindy, wait." Max stood.

"I didn't mean to say anything," Melissa protested. "Of course Storm can't really be *that* sick."

Cindy ran out of the cafeteria, her hands to her mouth. She stopped in front of a row of lockers and leaned against the cold metal, trying to take deep breaths. Her lungs felt too constricted to hold any air.

"Cindy." Max caught up to her and leaned against the lockers next to her. "Don't listen to Melissa. Maybe Storm just doesn't feel good—he might not be sick at all. And even if he is, he probably doesn't have equine infectious anemia." But Max's bright green eyes were worried.

Cindy felt a chill run through her entire body. *I'm not the only one who thinks Storm has equine infectious anemia—everybody does*, she thought. *I have to get back to him!*

"I—I can't talk to you now, Max," she choked out. "I have to go."

Cindy ran down the empty school halls to the office. "May I use the telephone to call home?" she asked Mrs. Krohn, the secretary. "I feel awful." *I'm sure not making that up*, she thought.

Her face must have been convincing because Mrs. Krohn quickly gestured at the phone. "Do you need to see the nurse?" she asked.

Cindy shook her head as she dialed Whitebrook's number, praying Ian would be home. She knew Beth had to work at her aerobics business in Lexington today. On the fifth ring Ian answered.

"Dad, I want to come home." The beige walls of the office blurred, and Cindy blinked back tears. "I feel so bad. . . . How's Storm?"

"He seems a little better," Ian said reassuringly. "Dr. Smith is coming out within the hour."

152

"Do you think you can come pick me up?" Cindy asked.

Ian hesitated. "Beth's here—I think she could come. I don't want to miss the vet."

"I thought Mom had to work." Something was very wrong. Cindy held her breath and gripped the phone tightly.

Ian sighed. "She stayed home in case I need help holding down the fort. If Storm does have something contagious, all hell is going to break loose around here. But we'll talk about it when you get here, sweetie. Your mom will be there in a few minutes."

On the drive home from school Cindy was silent. Beth patted Cindy's hand, but she was quiet, too. Cindy saw that her mom's face was etched with worry. *What's going to happen?* Cindy thought. It was hard for her to believe that just yesterday, she had been happily thinking about Storm's spring races. Now she just hoped he would live through the spring. *Today feels like a terrible nightmare!*

The instant the car stopped in the drive at Whitebrook, Cindy threw open the door and started running for Storm's stall. Whatever was wrong with him, she knew she needed to be with him.

He's not looking out of his stall, she thought frantically as she rushed down the training barn aisle. *He must be lying down. Dad probably only told me Storm was better so I wouldn't worry!*

Cindy looked in the stall. "Storm?" she said, her voice quavering.

153

Storm's stall was empty. Cindy stood frozen in shock and horror. Had Storm gotten so ill that he'd already been taken to the vet? Where could he be? Cindy dropped her head onto the half door. Her mind just wouldn't work.

She felt a hand on her shoulder. "Cindy, Storm's better than he was this morning, but I put him in the isolation barn as a precaution," Len said gently. "Dr. Smith just got here—she's outside talking with your dad."

Cindy swallowed hard. "Oh." The isolation stalls were in a small, attached building behind the training barn. It hurt to think of Storm being confined there all alone, so sick he had to be away from the other horses.

She turned and ran down the aisle to the back door of the training barn. Most of the horses in training were out in the paddocks, but Wonder's Champion and Limitless Time stuck curious heads over their doors. Cindy didn't stop to visit them. The pressure in her chest from anxiety and suppressed tears was almost squeezing out her breath.

The isolation barn was completely quiet. "Storm?" Cindy gasped, opening the door to the first stall. She tried to prepare herself to see the worst.

Storm was standing at the back of the stall, pointing his nose at the small, high window. The gray colt whickered when he saw her and walked energetically over to her. Then he tried to push past her out of the stall.

154

"No, no, you have to stay here for a little while," Cindy said, almost laughing with relief. Storm's nose was still running a little, but he seemed almost his old self. She hugged him tight around the neck. "You are better!"

She turned at the sound of voices. Ian and Dr. Smith came up behind her. "How is he?" Dr. Smith asked, stepping inside the stall. Storm nosed her medical bag dubiously, then quickly went to a corner of the stall.

"Easy, boy," Cindy said. She walked slowly over to Storm and gripped his halter so that Dr. Smith could examine him.

Ian and Dr. Smith were both looking hard at the colt. Cindy felt her heart sinking again at their grim expressions. "What's the matter?" she asked. "I thought he looked better."

"Yes, but he's definitely ill," Dr. Smith said. "I don't know what he has yet, but any infectious disease is potentially serious in a stable."

Cindy tried to keep Storm still while the vet completed her examination. The colt usually liked handling, but he had learned to associate Dr. Smith with unpleasant things like shots. "His temperature is elevated," Dr. Smith said finally. "But that could be symptomatic of any number of things."

Cindy noticed that she was readying a syringe. "Why are you taking blood?" Cindy asked. "He seems fine now except he has a little temperature." Storm was already backing up, trying to avoid the needle.

"I'm going to test him and all the other horses at Whitebrook for equine infectious anemia," Dr. Smith said slowly.

Cindy froze. Her mind was spinning with terror. She felt as if a deep hole had just opened up and swallowed her in its blackness.

Storm pulled his head from her limp fingers, but Cindy couldn't make herself move to get him back. She could only watch while Ian and Len restrained the colt so that Dr. Smith could take a blood sample. Storm rolled a pleading eye in her direction and wiggled away from the needle.

"Easy, boy," Cindy said automatically. As if in a dream she walked to Storm's side, steadying the colt with her hands and her voice. Storm relaxed at Cindy's touch, turning his head to make sure where she was. Cindy moved close so that the colt could see and smell her and so she could run both hands over his warm, satiny gray neck.

"I'll have the results first thing in the morning." Dr. Smith put the blood sample in her bag. "Let's do the other horses."

Cindy shook her head, wishing desperately that she hadn't heard those words. *Dr. Smith thinks all the horses are sick*, she realized. *Are they all going to die?*

14

Dr. Smith's face was grave as she shut the door to Storm's stall. "Why don't we take samples from the horses in training first?" she said. "Then we'll move on to the mares and the stallions."

Cindy turned away. She just didn't see how she could watch Dr. Smith test all the horses. "I want to see Glory," she choked out. If she could just see the other horse she loved so much, Cindy was sure she would feel better.

"Cindy, wash up very carefully first." Ian's mouth was set in a grim line. "We can't take the slightest chance of infecting the other horses."

Cindy stopped in her tracks. She realized that every time she went in to pet Storm now, she would have to thoroughly wash afterward. The disease was carried through blood and was usually transmitted by biting insects. But Cindy knew Dr. Smith wanted to be very careful. Cindy realized there was no escape from the danger hanging over the farm.

It's so hard to believe I have to scrub up after touching Storm, Cindy thought. *He's so beautiful—nothing has changed that!*

She walked slowly to the cottage to wash up. Cindy could have washed up at the barn, but she wanted to get away for a few minutes. All the sorrow and anxiety was upsetting her stomach again.

Beth was making sandwiches in the kitchen. "Oh, Cindy," she said softly. "Don't look so down. Things still may turn out all right."

"I don't know." Cindy dropped into a chair at the kitchen table and rested her cheek on the table's cool surface. Just the thought that anything could be wrong with Storm made her feel terrible.

"Are you going back down to the stable?" Beth asked.

"Yes." For the first time since she had lived at Whitebrook, Cindy didn't want to. But she knew she had to help in any way she could.

"Take these sandwiches for everybody down with you. I'll bring some drinks," Beth said.

"I'm not hungry." Cindy shrugged. "I bet nobody is."

"Even so, you should eat," Beth urged. "You'll have more strength to work with the horses."

"I just don't think I can," Cindy said. Her throat was so constricted, she could hardly swallow.

"Cindy, we'll pull through this," Beth said firmly.

Cindy lifted her head. "Do you really think so?"

Beth nodded. "We don't have a choice."

Cindy got up, pushing her hair out of her face. *Mom's right,* she thought. *I can't stay here moping.*

She washed up carefully at the kitchen sink and took the bag of sandwiches down to the training barn. Mike and Ashleigh's car was in the driveway. They had been out of town, looking at a colt they were thinking of buying. Cindy was sure they had driven home immediately when they received news of Storm's illness.

Dr. Smith, Ian, and Ashleigh were in Limitless Time's stall, taking a blood sample. The bay colt didn't like it at all. He squealed when the long needle went in and tried to lunge away. If Dr. Smith hadn't moved quickly with him, the needle would have broken off in his neck.

"Cindy." Ashleigh's face was drawn and white, but she tried to smile. "I'm glad you're here. We can use your help with Champion—he's next."

Cindy nodded. She had been afraid she wouldn't be able to handle it when Champion was tested. But Cindy drew courage from Ashleigh's brave expression.

"We left messages for Sammy," Ashleigh said as she opened Champion's stall door. "She should get word soon. Limitless Time probably would have behaved better if she'd been here."

"Yeah, he would have," Cindy said. She took a deep breath and walked into Champion's stall.

With a fiery snort the chestnut colt wheeled to face Cindy. "I know, you don't understand why you've been stuck in the barn so long," Cindy said, clipping a lead line to the dark brown colt's halter. "But this will just take a second, Champion—if you cooperate."

Dr. Smith uncapped the syringe and quickly slipped the needle into Champion's neck. The colt stood stoically, nibbling Cindy's hands. "He's not sensitive to needles like Limitless Time," Dr. Smith said. "That's a blessing with a colt as big and strong as this one."

Cindy patted Champion's neck. "Good boy! That's the way." *I think he's too feisty to be sick,* she tried to reassure herself.

Mike walked toward them from the office. Cindy's hopes plummeted again when she saw the expression on Mike's face. "I just got off the phone with Bill Dunlap at Pine Shadows Farm," he said.

Cindy remembered that was the farm Melissa had been talking about this morning at school. Melissa had said one of the horses there had tested positive for equine infectious anemia.

Cindy saw Ashleigh glance at her. Then Ashleigh shook her head at Mike.

They're trying to keep something from me! Cindy thought. "What is it?" she asked. "Please tell me what's happening, too."

"Okay," Mike said wearily. "You'll find out soon enough anyway. Pine Shadows had eleven horses total, and they all tested positive for the virus. All of them were put down this afternoon—six two- and three-year-olds in training, two broodmares and their foals, and the family's old pony."

"Every horse those people had." Cindy was numb with fear. "Were they all sick?"

Mike shook his head. "Only one of the mares. But since all the horses tested positive, they all had to be put down."

Just like here, Cindy thought. *Only Storm is sick!*

Ashleigh seemed to know what she was thinking. "Cindy, don't jump to conclusions," she said. "Even though I know it's hard not to."

"Why don't we move on to the mares' barn and try to finish up as quickly as we can?" Dr. Smith picked up her bag. Cindy could tell the vet was trying not to show any emotion.

"We can start with Wonder," Ashleigh said quietly. "I'll hold her."

Cindy's heart went out to Ashleigh. Ashleigh looked calm, but Cindy knew how much she must be suffering. Cindy knew that if Ashleigh could be brave about Wonder, she had to be brave about Storm, too. But Cindy's heart was breaking.

"I'll be back in a minute," she blurted, hurrying to the barn door.

"Cindy!" Ian called.

"Let her go," Ashleigh said.

Cindy ran through the stable yard and out onto the lane. She felt that she couldn't breathe. "I have to get away," she murmured. "I just can't stand it anymore!"

As she rushed by the mares' paddock, Fleet Goddess whinnied to her. A few of the other mares that hadn't yet been brought to the barn for testing whinnied, too. Cindy slowed as she heard the high voice of Fleet Goddess's brand-new foal, a stocky black filly named Fleet Street.

Shining hadn't had her foal yet. She was already up in the barn with Wonder, waiting to be tested. *Will Shining ever have her foal?* Cindy thought. *If she has to be put down, it will never even be born!*

Cindy's eyes stung with tears. The foal might never see the feathery new leaves of spring or smell the sweet scent of clover and grass. The world seemed to be bursting with life. *How can spring be a time of death?* she wondered.

Blinded by her tears, Cindy ran along the lane and through the woods. She sank onto her knees when she could run no farther, gasping for breath and sobbing.

At last she was spent. Cindy sat slowly back on her heels and realized where she was. "This is the meadow where I rode Storm with Max and Samantha," she said softly.

She remembered that day so clearly. Storm had pounded after the other horse, head up, mane and tail flying, lost in the pure joy of running. Cindy forgot her tears as she let the memories of Storm flood her mind.

Storm's sweet nature and beauty had struck her so powerfully the first time she saw him, at the July select yearling sale at Keeneland. Getting Storm had lifted her heart that day after Four Leaf Clover, an orphan colt Cindy had helped raise, had been sold at the same sale to Arabia.

Storm had been so easy to train. The confidence he had given her was a big reason, Cindy realized, that she could train a colt as difficult as Wonder's Champion.

Then there were Storm's races. He had run his heart out in every single race and shown beauty and dignity even in defeat. As a great sprinter, he had given her so many wonderful moments.

Cindy stood up resolutely and walked to the woods. She looked back toward the meadow. For a moment she thought she could see the dark gray colt running, his hooves barely touching the thick grass, his neck arched in triumph.

I have to go back home, Cindy said to herself, breaking into a run. *And I won't leave Storm again until we get through this—no matter what happens.*

15

"IT'S GOING TO BE A LITTLE LONESOME SLEEPING OUT here," Beth said as she slipped a pillow into a clean case. Ian helped arrange a blanket on a cot in Storm's stall. "I mean, before when you've slept out here, Len or one of your friends has been in the barn, too," Beth continued.

Cindy looked up. "I won't be lonesome," she said. "Storm and I have each other." Cindy knew that as long as she and the colt were together, she would never feel alone.

For the first time since that morning, when the nightmare with Storm had begun, Cindy felt sure she was doing the right thing. She had always stayed in the stall with Storm when she thought he needed her most, before his hardest races. She knew she belonged with him tonight.

Early tomorrow morning Dr. Smith would come out to Whitebrook with the test results. Cindy wanted to be in the barn so that she could hear the results immediately. She prayed Dr. Smith would tell her the horses were fine.

Storm was nudging straw around the stall with his nose, as if he were helping her prepare for bedtime. Cindy smiled a little. "Thanks, boy," she said. "We'll be comfortable, won't we?"

The colt stepped closer and whickered as if in agreement. Storm's charcoal coat gleamed under the soft barn lights. Looking at him now, Cindy was confident the news would be good tomorrow.

Beth smiled wanly. "Try to get a little sleep," she said. "Call up to the house if you need anything."

"I will." Cindy had brought the portable phone.

"Good night, Cindy," Ian said, looking over the stall door. He seemed worn out from the stress, and his eyes were worried as he looked from Cindy to the gray colt.

"Good night." Cindy leaned over the stall half door, watching until her dad shut the outside barn door. Storm joined her, as if he were seeing off their guest, too.

Cindy had always loved being alone with the horses at night. But tonight was different. The isolation barn was so quiet, and her frightening thoughts wouldn't go away. She was alone with Storm, who might be terribly sick, and with the threat hanging over the farm.

I wish I'd asked Heather to stay with me, Cindy thought. Heather had stopped by after school, as she had promised, but Cindy had been out in the meadow.

Storm shook himself and wandered restlessly around the stall. "I know, you want to get out," Cindy sympathized. *But how long will it be before you can?* she wondered. *Will you ever be allowed out again?*

Cindy tried to shake away her fears. It would be a long night, and she couldn't start thinking that way now. *I could call Heather.* Cindy picked up the phone.

Heather answered on the first ring. "I thought you might call," she said. "Oh, Cindy, I wish all this wasn't happening."

"Me too." Cindy glanced over at Storm. The colt had his head cocked and was staring at the phone. Cindy realized he had never seen one before. It was spooking him that people's voices were coming out of a small plastic thing. She scratched his ears reassuringly.

"How's Storm doing?"

"He seems fine." Cindy tickled the tip of the colt's nose.

"Well, that has to be a good sign," Heather said.

"I think so." Cindy tried to sound confident. "Can you come over again?"

"No." Heather sounded depressed. "My mom won't let me—I already asked. She says it's too late, but I bet she thinks I'll catch something from the horses."

"Dr. Smith says that's impossible," Cindy said.

"I know, but she'll never change her mind."

Heather sighed. "Listen, I'll be thinking about you. Call me the minute you know anything, okay?"

"I will." Cindy felt a little better, hearing the support in Heather's voice.

She hung up and sat down on the straw with her back against the wall. Storm walked over and bent his head to sniff her hands.

Cindy could feel the heavy quiet of the night and the isolated stable closing in on her again. "Max is always up late," she said to Storm. She picked up the phone again and punched in the Smiths' number. "Let's call him."

"Hello?" Max sounded wide awake.

"It's Cindy," she said.

"How are you doing?" Max asked. Cindy could hear the genuine concern in his voice.

"Not so well—I'm just so scared about Storm." This time the colt wasn't spooking from the phone. He was nosing it, as if he wanted to talk.

"Are you out in the barn with him?" Max asked.

Cindy smiled a little. "How did you guess? But it's not much fun," she said, her smile changing to a frown. "It's the isolation barn, and I'm all alone here. . . ."

"Do you want me to come over?" Max offered. "My mom's asleep, but I think she'd understand if I woke her up to give me a ride. She may be awake anyway. She's pretty tense about Storm, too."

"No, that's okay." Cindy didn't think it would be fair to disturb Dr. Smith when she had to get up so early. "Your mom's going to be over tomorrow morning anyway as soon as she gets the results back."

"I know." Max's voice was full of sympathy.

Cindy shifted the phone to her other ear. Storm was lipping it and had almost knocked it out of her hand. "I'd better go," she said. "I think Storm needs attention."

"Well, call again if you need to," Max said.

"Thanks." *I really have great friends,* Cindy thought as she hung up.

Storm was standing quietly, his head hanging a little. He looked sleepy to Cindy. Or maybe he was still sick. Cindy couldn't stand to see him that way.

"Let's play a game," she told the colt. "We should try to have some fun." She pulled a carrot out of her back pocket. "Here's half," she said, breaking the carrot in two and feeding him the big part. "You have to look for the other piece."

Cindy ran behind Storm. Before he could turn to see what she was doing, she hid the carrot under the straw. The first time she had to show him where it was, but then Storm caught on. The third time he wheeled quickly and grabbed the carrot before she could hide it.

"You win!" Laughing, Cindy let go of the carrot.

Storm's eyes were bright with the excitement of the game. He crunched the carrot and bobbed his head, asking to play again.

Cindy ran her fingers lightly over his neck. *This*

could be my last night with him, she thought. Suddenly the game wasn't fun anymore.

Cindy reached slowly under the blanket on her cot and brought out Storm's special saddlecloth that her family had given her for Christmas.

"Will you ever wear this again to a race?" she asked softly. Touching the cloth to her cheek, Cindy sank down onto the straw and wept bitterly.

In the morning Cindy stirred from an uneasy sleep. Sitting up slowly, she felt exhausted and disoriented. For a split second it seemed like a normal day, but then yesterday's terrible events came rushing back to her mind.

Storm was already standing by the stall door. "Morning, boy," Cindy said quietly. She opened the top of the door and looked out. The predawn sky was charcoal gray, the color of Storm's coat. "It's time to go to the track," she murmured. "You know that, too, don't you? But we won't be going today."

Cindy heard voices in the aisle of the barn. Ian, Mike, Dr. Smith, and Samantha were approaching the stall. Their faces were grim, and Cindy felt a sickening sense of dread.

"Cindy, I don't know how to tell you this." Ian hesitated. "I don't think there's any easy way."

"Are all the horses going to die?" Cindy asked. Her father's face was swimming before her eyes.

"No, they're not," Mike said. "The stallions, mares, and foals are all negative."

"Oh, thank God!" Cindy cried. Her thoughts had been so black all night, she could hardly believe the news was good. "But wait—what about the horses in training?"

"They're all fine, too," Samantha said. "Except . . ." Her voice faded, but Cindy saw Samantha's eyes turn to Storm. Cindy's heart began to beat faster.

"Cindy, sweetheart, the results were positive for Storm," Ian said gently. "He's the only one. I'm so sorry."

"No!" Cindy turned quickly to Storm and buried her face in his mane. He smelled clean and healthy, and his fur tickled her skin. Her heart was pounding. "Maybe the test results are wrong."

"I wish they were." Dr. Smith's face was filled with pity. "Cindy, I know how difficult this is to accept—"

"Storm will have to be put down," Mike said heavily. He leaned on the stall door and closed his eyes.

Cindy's mind was racing with fear. "But Storm's not even sick anymore! He doesn't have to be put down! I won't let you!"

Cindy beat her fists on the wood door of the stall. She hardly knew she was screaming, but Storm had fled to the back of his stall. "Please don't kill him! You can't!"

"Cindy, Cindy—stop!" Ian gripped her hands. "Listen to me. Equine infectious anemia isn't usually fatal, but Storm will never get over it. He'll never race again, and he could spread it to the other horses. They tested negative—but only for now."

"So we'll keep Storm in the isolation barn," Cindy said haltingly through her sobs. "He doesn't have to be around the other horses!"

"That's no kind of life for a racehorse." Samantha's voice was choked with tears. "Cindy, to keep Storm alive, we'd have to quarantine him for life. And even then we'd still be putting the other horses at risk."

Storm walked up from the back of his stall and nudged Cindy timidly. He seemed to be asking if she was all right.

Cindy wept into his gray neck. *What can I do? I can't let you put Glory, Shining, and all the other Whitebrook horses in danger,* she thought. "You wouldn't want that, would you, boy?" she asked, her voice shaking. "And I can't lock you up for the rest of your life."

Cindy dropped her arms and looked at her horse, seeing every inch of him. From his small, perfectly shaped ears to his luxurious gray tail, he was all strength, grace, and beauty. *He's the fastest horse in the world,* Cindy thought in a daze. *How can anybody kill him?*

"I want you here," she said unsteadily. "I can't stand to be without you." Storm lovingly nuzzled Cindy's hand as her tears fell.

"Cindy, please—you're just making it worse on yourself by waiting," Ian pleaded.

"I can't leave Storm," Cindy sobbed. "I just can't!"

"Let's go see Glory and Shining," Samantha said. Cindy looked up and saw her older sister's tears.

Cindy shook her head. Glory and Shining seemed in another world—she only wanted to be in this stall. "I'm supposed to take care of you, Storm," she whispered. "How can I do that if I leave you?"

"Leave her be for a while," Len said. His face was sadder than Cindy had ever seen it.

For hours Cindy clung tightly to Storm, sobbing into his soft mane. Cindy's cheeks were red and swollen from crying. Storm stood very still, as if he understood her distress and wanted to help.

"Cindy." Cindy looked up through a thick blur of tears and saw Ashleigh. Ashleigh slipped into the stall and stood beside her. She rested a hand on Storm's shoulder. "Say good-bye to him," she said quietly.

Cindy let out a trembling sigh. "No."

"You have to." Tears streaked Ashleigh's face, but her voice was sure and soothing.

Ashleigh knows how I'm feeling, Cindy thought. *She knows what it's like to lose your horse. I have to do this!*

But a knife twisted in her heart as she turned to the beautiful colt. "This doesn't mean I don't love you, Storm," she said, her words broken by sobs. "Because I do—forever, and that's a promise! I'm doing it for you, boy. You can't live like this. Please understand!"

Storm stepped closer and put his head trustingly in Cindy's arms. Cindy hugged him hard one last time, holding his soft neck against her wet face.

"Cindy." Ashleigh's voice was very gentle. "It's time to go."

"I can't." Cindy shook her head, her eyes blinded by tears.

"Come with me." Ashleigh took Cindy's hand, and they walked to the door together. Cindy heard Storm's last, soft whicker as she left the stall.

16

TWO DAYS LATER CINDY STOOD BY THE MARES' PADDOCK, watching the new foals romp in the crystal clear spring air. Seven foals had been born so far. Their black, brown, chestnut, and gray coats were a lovely accent to the acres of brilliant green grass in the paddock. The foals were a nice selection of coat colors, Cindy thought. Almost every possible color for a Thoroughbred was represented.

Shining's foal had been born yesterday. She was a gorgeous, almost black filly and looked a lot like her sire, Chance Remark. Townsend Princess's filly had been born a week ago. Already spirited and active, the little bay filly was chasing two colts at the back of the paddock.

Cindy sighed heavily and dropped her chin on the second board of the fence. The foals were beautiful and lively, but nothing helped to take her mind off Storm's death.

Cindy had just come from the training barn. The gray colt's empty stall had gaped at her, a hole that wouldn't fill.

"Hey, Cindy." Ashleigh walked over to the fence with Mike.

"Hi." Looking at their sad faces, Cindy remembered how much they had loved Storm, too—Ashleigh as his jockey, and Mike with his intense admiration of sprinters.

"How are you feeling?" Ashleigh asked.

"Not too good." Cindy looked out at the paddock. Shining's filly had gotten up her courage and walked a few steps away from her mother. "I just keep remembering how fast Storm was." *This is the first time in days I've been able to talk without crying,* she thought. It felt good to be around Ashleigh and Mike.

"He was a brilliant star that flamed and quickly faded." Ashleigh nodded. "I know how you feel, Cindy."

"It's just not fair," Cindy burst out. "Storm always tried his hardest . . . he was the sweetest horse on the farm. Why did something have to happen to him?"

"I don't know, Cindy." Ashleigh rubbed her forehead.

"Was it our fault?" Cindy asked hoarsely. She had tormented herself with that question since Storm's death. "Dr. Smith said stress makes a horse to be susceptible to illness. Storm ran so hard every time he raced. . . ."

"Cindy, this wasn't anyone's fault," Ashleigh said.

"I'm sure of that." She hesitated. "Somehow it just wasn't meant to be that Storm would live, the way he wasn't meant to be a distance runner. I know it's not fair."

"You'll always have your memories of him," Mike said gently.

That's the problem, Cindy thought, fighting tears. Every time she let her mind wander for an instant, she remembered something about Storm—the proud way he carried his head, the soft look in his eyes when he saw her.

"I really do know what you're going through." Ashleigh bowed her head for a moment, then looked at Cindy. "We lost half of the horses at our farm, Edgardale, when I was a few years younger than you. It was so terrible, Cindy. Every day more of them would get sick. And every day more of them would die."

Cindy looked at Ashleigh with surprise and sympathy. Cindy knew the story of Edgardale, which Samantha had heard from Ashleigh's parents. Samantha had said Ashleigh never talked about it.

How did Ashleigh live through that? Cindy wondered.

"But we have to move on," Ashleigh continued. "I know it seems impossible right now. But so many good things will happen in your life, Cindy. You have to let go of your sadness and pain."

"Right now you'd better get Champion for his exercise," Mike said, managing a smile. "He's throwing a fit up in the barn. Vic tried to take him out, but Champion nipped him."

Cindy wiped away her tears and took a deep breath. She had to go get Champion, or he would be in major trouble again. "Okay," she said. "But I think I'll just walk him—I don't have time to do anything else before school." Cindy knew she had time to ride if she hurried, but since Storm's death she hadn't felt like riding. She had put Champion out in the paddock yesterday, and he had just stood around. *I can't let him down,* she thought.

As Cindy walked away from the paddock she heard the soft thunder of hooves. Turning, she saw the foals running swiftly in a pack, a cloud of bright colors. Small as they were, the exquisite young Thoroughbreds felt their heritage to run and were already fast. Princess's foal was in the lead as they charged to the back of the paddock, swerved in unison like a school of fish, and galloped to the front gate to visit Ashleigh and Mike.

"I've got to name them," Cindy said aloud. Since she had come to Whitebrook, Cindy had named most of the foals. Everyone thought she had a real knack for it.

In the training barn Wonder's Champion was alone. The dark brown colt was peering anxiously out of his stall. When he saw Cindy, he whinnied shrilly.

"Have you been waiting long?" Cindy asked. "I'm sorry, boy."

Champion sniffed her hands, then tossed his head and let fly with a kick to the boards of his stall.

"Stop that—you'll hurt yourself." Cindy took him out of the stall. She crosstied him in the aisle and picked up a brush.

"Thought you might be up," Len commented, coming out of the stable office. "I brought Champion in from the paddock half an hour ago."

Cindy nodded. "I'll take him out for a walk. Then maybe I'll ride him a little on the track."

"Sounds good." Len's expression was kindly. Everyone at Whitebrook had been so nice to her since Storm's death, Cindy thought gratefully. They had put aside their own sorrow to comfort her.

Cindy headed down the aisle to visit Storm's empty stall again. Sometimes, if she sat in the stall and closed her eyes, she could pretend that he was only away at the track and that he'd come home soon.

Champion whinnied. Cindy looked back and saw that he was yanking on the crossties, trying to pull them out of the wall. "Hold still, Champion!" Cindy ran back to him. "All right, already—we'll go outside!" Cindy couldn't help smiling a little at the colt's high spirits.

Champion marched across the stable yard a step ahead of Cindy. "No, I don't want to go to the track," Cindy said, turning him. "Not now. Let's just walk on the lane. And walk *behind* me, Champion—I decide where we go." She stopped the colt to make her point.

The dark colt stood still, his almost black eyes alert. He sniffed the wind.

"A walk will be good for you," Cindy said, straightening the colt's thick mane on the right side of his neck. She kept him standing just a few seconds longer to make sure he understood who was in charge. "We'll go back to our regular exercise soon—I promise. So settle down."

Champion followed her to the lane at a sedate walk. He seemed to realize that his exercise would be a walk today, not a run.

Cindy felt guilty again, but her thoughts wandered back to Storm. She dreaded the thought of riding Champion, then not having Storm to ride. Storm had been the focus of her hopes and happiness for so long.

Champion gave a sharp snort as a tiny bird carrying nesting material flew brazenly by his nose. The big colt stopped in his tracks, then jumped several times in place, kicking up his heels.

"You and that bird feel good, don't you?" Cindy ran her fingers over the colt's neck. Champion's coat was thicker than Storm's. Storm's silky fur had felt almost like a cat's. Champion's dense coat felt like a closely woven Oriental carpet.

Champion doesn't know there's anything to be sad about, Cindy thought as she walked with the colt into the woods. *He loves the spring, and being outside, and just being alive.*

The trees had burst into a riot of soft green leaves, filling the holes between the branches in the forest. Delicate purple and white wildflowers nestled thickly at the trees' roots. Cindy stopped and picked a bouquet of them.

"I know what I have to do," she said to the colt. Cindy led him to Storm's grave.

Storm was buried in the meadow where he had run his last race, against Daly Bar Dun. Cindy had suggested that Storm be buried there, but she had been unable to make herself watch the burial or visit the grave.

The meadow was bright with new clover and grass. *Storm's grave will be an ugly brown patch in the middle of so much green*, Cindy thought, feeling sick. *I'm not going to be able to do this.*

Champion pulled her firmly ahead. Either he was determined to make her follow through on her plan or he thought she was stopping to take him back to the barn. Cindy halfheartedly pulled on his lead rope, but she didn't have the strength to make him walk behind her.

She saw the grave, tucked into a corner of the meadow. But it wasn't a bare spot in a field of green, Cindy saw with wonder. Daffodils and other spring flowers bloomed brightly in the dirt. Cindy remembered that Samantha had told her she'd planted flowers on the grave. As Cindy bent to smell the flowers' sweet scent, her heart went out to her sister in gratitude for that nice gesture.

Cindy knelt beside the grave and touched the soft dirt, then a white lilac. Gently she laid her own bouquet between the other flowers.

Cindy bowed her head. For a moment her feelings

threatened to overwhelm her. Storm was gone, when she had thought he would be there forever to love. But he had been just a flash in her life; as Ashleigh had said, a precious spark that had all too soon gone out. Cindy turned away from the grave in wrenching sorrow.

She remembered Storm's last day of victory, in the Breeders' Cup Sprint Championship at Gulfstream. *He was so glorious, so proud—and so perfect*, Cindy thought, her heart aching. It was as if he had been so perfect, he had flown out of her life to heaven—or into her memories, where he would always run.

I'll love him forever, she thought as her tears fell onto the grave. *Just the way I promised him.*

Champion had lowered his head to nibble one of the flowers. Suddenly he swung his head around and rudely pushed her with his nose.

The eager expression in his eyes and the brilliant beauty of the day made Cindy smile through her tears. "You've had enough of standing around, haven't you?" she asked. *I haven't ridden Champion in two days*, she thought. *He's going to be a monster when I get back on him!*

"All right, boy," she said, running her hand down his deep brown neck. Champion was already moving ahead of her with light, spirited strides. "We'd better get out on the track. It's time to go."

Joanna Campbell was born and raised in Norwalk, Connecticut and grew up loving horses. She eventually owned a horse of her own and took riding lessons for a number of years, specializing in jumping. She still rides when possible and has started her three-year-old granddaughter on lessons. In addition to publishing over twenty-five novels for young adults, she is the author of four adult novels. She has also sung and played piano professionally and owned an antique business. She now lives on the coast of Maine in Camden with her husband, Ian Bruce. She has two children, Kimberly and Kenneth, and three grandchildren.

Karen Bentley rode in English equitation and jumping classes as a child and in Western equitation and barrel racing classes as a teenager. She has bred and raised Quarter Horses and, during a sojourn on the East Coast, owned a half-Thoroughbred jumper. She now owns a red roan registered Quarter Horse with some reining moves and lives in New Mexico. She has published nine novels for young adults.

created by Joanna Campbell

Read all the books in the Thoroughbred series and experience the thrill of riding and racing, along with Ashleigh Griffen, Samantha McLean, Cindy McLean, and their beloved horses.